VALENA

Valena

NORAH MCMENAMON

Published in British Columbia, Canada in 2015 by
Meadow House Publishing
18829 122 Avenue
Pitt Meadows, v3y 2k6

Copyright © 2006 Norah McMenamon
Cover and artwork by Valerie Hocking copyright ©
Meadow House Publishing ® 2015

Library and Archives Canada Cataloguing in Publication

McMenamon, Norah, author

Valena / Norah McMenamon, Valerie Hocking.

Issued in print and electronic formats.

isbn 978-0-9938724-0-2 (bound).— isbn 978-0-9938724-1-9 (pdf)

I. Hocking, Valerie, author II. Title.

ps8625.m46 v35 2015   jC813'.6   c2015-903817-0
                                      c2015-903818-9

Design and layout by Vancouver Desktop Publishing Centre
Printed and bound in the US by IngramSpark

ACKNOWLEDGMENTS

Thank you to my dear friend and editor, Homer Powell, for his patience, guidance, and loving encouragement on this book. And a special "thank you" for the contribution of your wisdom for sharing past memories on life itself.

I would like to acknowledge, too, Valerie Ann Hocking, without her the story would have never been dreamed up.

For their help in keeping my heart grounded through laughter and love, thank you to my dear children Nicole and Curtis.

*This book is dedicated with love to
Homer Powell, and my children, Valerie, Nicole,
and Curtis. Also loving memories of my immediate
family, the late Kermack McMenamon, Kathryn
McMenamon, and my brother John.*

Table of Contents

ONE

Zymurgy / 11

TWO

The Royal Nightmare / 19

THREE

ECAE / 77

FOUR

The Secret / 131

FIVE

Flower Petal Cottage / 145

SIX

The Garden Shed / 156

SEVEN

Gypsy Magic / 178

EIGHT

The Forest / 199

NINE

The Tainted Knight / 254

TEN

The Hair Ball / 293

ELEVEN

Gypsy / 359

ONE

✦

Zymurgy

In a far away land, high above a hidden forest, stood the old castle of Zymurgy. It was the noblest castle in the land. On this cold stormy night, wind and frozen rain tore at the thick vines that clung to the high stone walls. Darkness came as the wind harshly thrust a large rusted old chain upward, smashing a magnificent stained glass lantern down into the dirty and icy waters of the moat that encircled the castle walls.

High up in a tall tower of the castle a beautiful stained glass window was aglow. Shadows moved quickly back and forth across it and erratically from top to bottom. Was the great Knight of Zymurgy in trouble?

In a huge fireplace the flames filled the tower room with the smell of sweet burning maple sap. As the roaring fire cast a bright orange flickering glow into the cold stone walled room, the great Knight of Zymurgy took his stance, holding up his arm. Why, it was only little Sir Benjamin Bailey the Third, a four-year-old boy depicting a grand knight, indeed, bravely defending himself against his imaginary fearsome opponent.

Sir Benjamin Bailey's skinny little body flailed about inside his nightshirt, which caught the draft from the castle's cold cobble-stone floor. His large grey eyes reflected so much glow from the fire that they would scare even the largest mouse away. His soft curly black hair fell upon his frail shoulders and down his back, casting dramatic dancing shadows upon his grandfather's tower room walls.

As the fire crackled in the huge fireplace and a wintry wind whistled its way through the crevices in the stone walls and under the doorways, young Bailey fiercely fought his opponent. Bright flashes of lightening sil-houetted the large stained glass window, and quickly after that a booming roll of thunder stopped the boy. Whirling around, he gazed in fear at the flashing heavens.

"Grandfather, grandfather!" he yelled. "I am a great knight, I will protect you!" And with a throaty cry of attack, he pointed his imaginary sword towards his foe.

Grandfather took his favourite seat in his big wooden storytelling throne right beside the fireplace. He used his wrinkled bony old hands to lower his tall thin frame into the centre of the chair then rested his large head of long white locks, which fell majestically along the sides of his kind weathered face.

As his grandson fought and played, the kind-hearted king gazed fondly at a dainty wooden throne sitting across from his chair. A fine piece of art, he thought to himself. On the back of the chair were delicately carved sweet peas in the shape of a 'V' and it had a soft purple cushion upon which the queen would often sit in the evenings with him and rest. He continued to look about the room. Over the soot-ridden fireplace was a display of dark grey armour. The most prominent piece was a large heavy sword, the handle adorned with flowers which were also in the shape of a large 'V'.

The old king bowed his head. "Memories

that only a chivalrous knight could make sense of," he said sadly, under his breath.

Grandfather's failing eyes were growing tired. He gazed towards his grandson and admired young Bailey's will to be so courageous. As the old king fell into a slumber, a dream fragment brought back the memory of a young knight, eyes sparkling and alive with fear, bringing an evil knight to his knees.

Grandfather was not the only one retiring for the evening, for under his throne was his aged cat whom he called Gypsy. She could eat the fish right off your plate then stare at you like she'd caught it for herself. Gypsy had a dirty, scruffy white coat. Her grey nose was dry and cracked, and her purple and yellow kaleidoscope eyes were partially covered by her sparse feather-like tail as she lay curled up in a tight ball trying to sleep.

Suddenly the largest boom of thunder shook the tower. "Ah!" Bailey cried out and ran to his grandfather, jumping onto his lap. The old man had dozed off. "Grandfather, wake up," the child pleaded, as he pulled on one of his ears. "Wake up, wake up!"

Grandfather's eyes popped open wide,

he looked around. "We're all awake now, Bailey," he scolded. "What has frightened you so?"

"The big noise from out there," Bailey said, pointing towards the dark stained glass window, the rain now falling gently outside. He turned back to look at his grandfather while digging his feet down into the sides of the cushion and putting his skinny stick-like arms around the old man's neck. Then, looking into his eyes, he said, "When I grow up I'm going to be a very brave knight and ride a really big horse. I'm going to protect you, Grandfather. I'm going to wear a shiny metal suit and carry a big sword. I will be a great hero."

The king listened carefully to his grandson. He could see the noble eyes of a knight in the making. "Bailey," he said, reaching to hold his grandson's tiny hand. "Listen carefully to me. The man who wears the shiny suit is not a hero but a fool."

The child crooked his head to one side and frowned, too young to understand the old man's wise message. He then pointed to the display of armour above the mantel.

"Grandfather, could I please just try one of your swords? Please? Maybe I could try that one, the big sword with all the flowers and the 'V' on it. I like flowers."

Grandfather frowned then focused his eyes upon the splendid display. "What is up there on that wall must stay there," he said sternly.

"Why do you frown when you look up there?" the child asked. "Is it bad stuff?" Grandfather lowered his eyes and bowed his head slowly.

"Are you sad, Grandfather?" Bailey asked.

Remembering an ancient battle, the old man shook his head from side to side then let out a heavy sigh.

"All you do is look up there, then close your eyes and fall asleep," Bailey complained.

"Oh, is that what I do?" Grandfather said, coming out of his slump.

"Yes," the child answered. Then, leaning in close, he whispered in a pleading voice, "Can you please tell me a great hero story?" Young Bailey looked closely at his grandfather's gnarled arms; then, with one of his small hands, he reached out and gently touched the ancient scars.

"Tell me the story of how you were captured by those evil men, and how you got those little red dots all over your arms."

He pointed at one and wrinkled up his little nose. "How long did it take you to pull out all those yucky things? Do they still hurt?"

"Oh, that's another story," Grandfather grumbled. "I'll tell that story some other night."

"And tonight?" Bailey perked up.

Grandfather looked down at his grandson, then a twinkle of a smile crossed his wrinkled old face as he held up his index finger and pressed it gently against the side of his nose in a classic 'I'm thinking' gesture. He pondered carefully, then, "I know!" he announced. "I will tell you a story of a great hero, but you, my little Benjamin Bailey the Third, you must promise me that you will never raise a sword to another man's heart."

Bailey hung down his little head, fearing his knighthood days were gone forever. Then, with sad grey eyes, he looked at his grandfather and slowly swung his head from side to side a couple times then up and down a couple times. He said nothing, but he understood.

His grandfather was very wise, and Bailey knew that he meant what he said about swords and a man's heart.

The rain persisted, falling gently upon the towers of Zymurgy as the warm embers from the fireplace continued to glow.

"Now, close your eyes my child and listen," Grandfather said in a gentle voice, holding the little boy close in his arms. "Many long years ago, many very long years before you were born," the old king poked a finger at the child with gentle affection and then began to tell one of the most wonderful hero stories of his time, the widespread legend of the infamous 'Tainted Knight'.

TWO

The Royal Nightmare

Thomas Alexander Horribin, the young and handsome King of Zymurgy, had taken the hand of Catherine Samuels as his wife. Catherine was the only daughter of Sir Michael Samuels, the wealthiest and most influential citizen of Zymurgy. Catherine was certainly not a beauty. Nor was she dainty and graceful. She had been spoiled as a child and was accustomed to getting anything and everything she wanted. Except, so far, she had never gained amorous admiration from a young man for her natural charm and beauty, which, with Catherine, was highly lacking.

In the spring of their second year of marriage Catherine joyously discovered she was pregnant, but soon experienced unbearable back pain and relentless morning sickness. At the beginning of the last month the living and growing thing inside her began a torrent of kicking for long periods of time, as if in an angry rage. Even at night the absurd thing kicked for hours. Finally, after several months of mental and physical torment, Catherine finally gave birth to a shrivelled, angry looking male baby with a jagged ear-splitting cry. They gave him the name of Erick Cornelius Horribin.

After only one week, the duty of mothering this endlessly demanding newborn baby was so unnerving that the young queen delegated all care of the child to the royal nursery staff; six competent women, including several wet nurses to provide an overabundant amount of breast milk for the infant. The staff kept their mouths closed while diligently overworking themselves to keep their jobs as long as possible. Their duties entailed a strictly prodigal upbringing of the royal infant, but they didn't hesitate to spoil him rotten and grant him his every wish.

During the next three years Catherine learned that her husband, the king, really did love and respect her, and her nature softened considerably. When she found herself pregnant once again, she discovered beauty and peace within herself. She gave birth to another son and this baby came into the world with the smile of an angel upon his handsome face. They proudly named him Isaac Nathan Horribin.

Seven years later the king and queen were blessed with the birth of their third child, a baby girl. This sweet red-haired infant had a playful nature but, being sadly over pro-tected, lacked natural intuition. They named her Remoh Sylvia Horribin.

In stark contrast to how she dealt with Erick when he was born, Catherine devoted all her love and attention to her younger chil-dren, particularly when they were babies, as did the king and most of the staff. Young Prince Erick was sharply, resentfully aware of this. He would hide himself away in secret places of the castle for hours and brood over this, seeing their actions as spiteful. He would entertain dark fantasies of how, one day, he was going to make sure they all knew of his ill feelings.

After a dozen or so years young Prince Erick Horribin turned out to be a spoiled

teenage brat who ran roughshod over anything that displeased him, especially his
younger brother Isaac, who, from the
moment of his birth, made Erick irreconcil-
ably jealous. He developed an uncontrollable
hatred for him. Even before this Erick had
shown an aggressive nature. He was totally
self-absorbed and would explode in an angry
rage when not given what he wanted, or
was prohibited from doing what he'd set his
mind to. He especially hated it when King
Thomas, his father, would scold him in the
presence of onlookers.

But earlier, before that, before Isaac was
born, Erick loved those moments just before
bedtime when his sleeping chamber seemed
dark and deathly scary. His eyes would
grow wide with excitement as his father sat
upon his bed telling him dreadful stories of
the blood-bathed battles he engaged in as a
youth, and how his now diminished army
had fearlessly defended his kingdom from
invading warriors. Then, after many terrible years of vicious fighting, these barbaric
intruders were finally driven out and peace
came to the land.

The child was mesmerized. Gripped with excitement by the image, he easily saw himself as a valiant warrior fighting off the dreaded enemy. "You must keep yourself strong," the king would tell him, pointing his finger at his three-year-old son, "for one day you will become a great king."

That sparked a fantasy that became Erick's favourite, a fantasy that became deeply rooted in his fertile young brain. He loved imagining himself standing on a hilltop dressed in full battle armour, his one and only true friend—his shining sword—gripped tightly. With intense valour he jabbed and slashed at the enemy. Then after the battle, after victory, sitting on his throne in the royal court with the jewelled crown on his head and the white and purple royal robe draped artfully over his body, King Erick Horribin would dispatch stern justice to those who had opposed him or who might oppose him. "To the dungeon with him!" he would command. And then the guards would drag some unfortunate peasant off to the torture chamber below.

Through his growing adolescent years the young prince developed a challenging and combative attitude toward his father, which angered the king greatly—he hated having his authority challenged by his own son or to be the object of his deliberate show of disrespect, often in public. The relationship between them never improved. By numerous accounts it seemed the cocky young Prince Erick would exploit any opportunity to make things worse between them.

Haughty Prince Erick's behaviour infected everyone and his devious thoughts would drive him to constantly create turmoil in the life of his sweet sister, Remoh. When she was only five years old she was in the stables with Annette Gray, a charming blue-eyed, dark-haired young girl whose family were close friends of the king and queen. Annette, a happy-go-lucky girl, was the same age as Prince Isaac, and in return for boarding her beautiful horse at Zymurgy stables she eagerly agreed to teach the incredibly horse shy Remoh to ride a small arthritic old mare named Sugar.

On this particular visit Annette had brought Remoh a delicious apple scone and instructed her to eat it outside the stable. Remoh took one look at old Sugar and gave the decrepit mare a grin as if to say, 'maybe tomorrow', then off she skipped towards the two big open doors at the back of the stable.

Just a hundred feet outside those same doors, a big mean brown and black wild coyote was sleeping. The king had named this beast Storm, because he was as unpredictable as the raging storm that had moved across the land with hail, thunder and lightning on the night they had found him. The king had heard his horses kicking in the stables and making loud neighing sounds so he sent a servant to see what the ruckus was about. The frightened servant found the crazed coyote running wildly around inside the stable.

They never found out how he had come to be there but the animal had since been chained and kept under a covered area out back of the stables to frighten intruders. The coyote was well fed with table scraps and spent his time sleeping inside a big wooden kennel. Lucky for him King Thomas had a soft spot in his heart for animals.

Today was no different from any other day and, as usual, Prince Erick was up to no good, sneaking about, spying on the girls from behind the back doors of the stable. He saw Remoh was not paying attention and was skipping eagerly towards the open back doorway while looking down into her hands at her treat. As Erick waited for her he lurched his head and upper body back, held on to the wooden door latch, and swung the door forward just enough so that as Remoh came through the doorway she wouldn't see him. He grabbed the end of the door with both hands so as not to lose his balance and swung one of his long legs out, kicking his sister's small hands with the tip of his boot, sending the apple biscuit up into the air. A few tiny finches landed, then quickly fled after retrieving the fresh apple and crumbs that lay scattered upon the ground. The commotion awakened Storm. As young naive Remoh ran to save her biscuit, the startled coyote instantly got up and raced to protect his territory, biting the baby finger from her left hand and leaving her bleeding and screaming. Finally she collapsed to the ground in shock.

Annette was startled by Remoh's high-pitched screams. She turned around and saw the coyote, picked up a pitchfork and started charging towards the animal, yelling to scare him away. The coyote yelped and backed off with its tail between its legs.

Seeing what happened Prince Erick ran around the side of the stable to hide, then, getting an idea, he ran out into the royal vegetable garden where a humble servant was hard at work. Erick quickly removed his brown leather vest and put it on the servant. He told him he could have it as a royal keepsake. Once Erick had gained his composure he snuck around to the front of the stable and looked in through the wide open front doors. He saw Annette at the opposite end, outside the open back doorway, down on her knees beside Remoh. It was then that Prince Erick realized his devious plan was about to give him an excellent opportunity to get out of trouble. Suddenly he ran in through the stable towards Annette to help her rescue Remoh, not letting on that he knew what had happened earlier.

"I was walking by the stable and heard a shrill scream. What's happened?" Erick asked.

"Remoh has been bitten by the coyote,"

cried Annette. Then, like a hero, the sly prince picked up his frail, bleeding young sister in his arms and carried her back towards the castle. Annette ran ahead to get help and, as Erick approached the castle's kitchen doors, an odd-looking hunch-backed servant woman saw them coming, opened the door, then screamed for someone to get the doctor.

After taking Remoh into a small room that smelled of medicine, Erick laid her on a cot. A servant held a cool cloth to her clammy forehead while the palace doctor stopped the bleeding and removed pieces of gravel from her left hand where the little finger was mutilated. Her right hand, bruised and swollen from being kicked, had been put to soak in a clay pot with cool water and fine herbs from the garden. Annette, feeling helpless, was called into the medical room along with Erick. The queen sat at her sweet young daughter's side and gently caressed her slender arm. Remoh winced in pain and wouldn't speak. The distraught queen waited to hear what had happened. Annette began to explain that earlier on, while grooming her horse, she saw someone through the crack in the back stable doors wearing a white shirt and a brown leather vest. He was back there doing something but Annette had just kept to herself, minding her own business, and continued working.

The queen looked at Erick. He didn't add anything to Annette's explanation.

"Don't you own a brown leather vest, Erick?" insinuated his mother.

"Yes, but…I can explain!" Erick blurted.

"And you will," she replied.

The queen immediately sent for her husband the king to deal with the situation.

In no time, the king himself escorted his son Erick through the castle towards a tall tower where, inside, they climbed a narrow staircase that led them high up to the king's private study room. Along the way King Thomas preached honesty and nobility. After reaching the landing at the top of the tower's long winding stairwell a guard approached them, unlocked a heavy creaky wooden door, and opened it. Suddenly a wild black crow cawed loudly, flapped it's wings, and flew past them to find freedom. The spooked men entered the big round stone-walled room with its massive fireplace, where old pieces of armour were displayed majestically over the mantel.

The gentle morning sun shone on the magnificent stained glass window of the tower and colours were cast about the room. A small section along the wall had old books stacked up against it, some had fallen over onto the edge of a piece of worn red velvet that had crinkled up underneath them. A huge slab of rock used as a table stood underneath the stained glass window where unrolled maps and scrolls lay flat, held by solid gold paper weights.

King Thomas entered the room first. He approached a large wooden throne and sat upon it with a stern look on his face. Erick followed and stood before him at ease, trying to portray innocence before telling the story he'd thought up earlier.

"Erick. Be honest. What happened to your sister?" King Thomas asked.

Erick knew that Annette had mentioned someone hanging around out back of the stable in a brown leather vest. His initial plan might work because of her lack of attention.

"Well…early this morning, before Annette had arrived," he told his father, "I removed my fancy brown leather vest, the one with the gold buttons that grandfather Samuels gave to me. I hung it over the rail of my horse's stall then took my horse for an early morning jaunt…out into the forest…so I could…bird watch."

Beneath the king's furrowed brow he stared at his son. He knew that Erick was as quick at lying as time was at passing.

Erick continued, "When I returned…my vest was gone! All the exercise made me hungry, so…I…went for breakfast. Later, being concerned as to the whereabouts of my vest, I…decided to go for a walk to the stables to look around and I spotted the head servant wearing it out in the garden, like he was the king himself! I started towards him, then heard a shrill scream from the stables. Running to the front doors I saw Annette out through the back doors, on her knees beside Remoh, who was injured and laying on the ground."

Shifty-eyed Erick glanced toward the floor, faking a concerned look, trying to trick his father into believing him. When he was finished the king told him to stand and wait outside the tower room door. Erick's story seemed to make sense but the king couldn't find a single reason to trust him. Right away the king sent his guard to bring him the servant whom Erick saw wearing his vest, so he could be questioned.

"This can't be!" King Thomas growled in disbelief, for the ageing servant had a good reputation and had worked hard around the castle for many years. King Thomas was torn and suffered inward anger towards himself for doubting his own good judgement.

The humble servant arrived, puzzled as to why he was brought to the tower room high up in the castle where he'd never been allowed before. He became frightened and trembled. Tears filled his eyes as the guard positioned him to stand in front of the king, who then questioned him about the incident. The servant nervously explained himself, then knelt down on the hard cobblestone floor and told His Majesty that Prince Erick gave him the vest as a keepsake. Taking the vest off he offered it back to the king, begging for forgiveness. The king gently took the vest from the meek servant and asked the guard standing by the door to bring Erick back into the room with them. The king's blood boiled in anger. Erick entered the room and stood beside the servant who was still kneeling on the floor. Holding the vest up in front of them, the king asked his son once more if he'd given the servant his vest. Looking down and scowling at the innocent servant, Erick breathed,

"Who would do that? . . ."

The king gave Erick back his vest and dismissed him.

That same evening the king felt ill and was sick to his stomach after sentencing the ageing servant man to one meal a day and life in the dungeon and leaving his absent-minded son—thirteen-year-old Shway, the royal's errand boy—broken-hearted.

Remoh finally recovered many months later, after being deathly ill with high temperatures caused by a viral infection from the filthy dog bite. Her first mumbled words were, "Why did Erick hurt me?" Neither the queen nor the doctor could make out what the weak little girl was saying and later on, being so young, she could only recall bits and pieces of what had happened. Finally the sickly-looking bony young girl rose from her bedside and walked for the first time since the incident, with a special walking stick to help her get around. She was seventy-five-percent blind in both eyes. The palace doctor had sadly informed the king and queen that their daughter would never see effectively again.

Erick, upon his mother's orders, had only to take his father's so-called pet, the coyote, and put it back into the wilderness where it belonged.

Queen Catherine had long ago stifled the small amount of mothering instinct she may have had in earlier times, but now, with her first-born son a boisterous, rowdy and disrespectful young teenager, shouting and making harsh demands, she would cry out angrily at him, "You are a wicked, unfeeling, royal nightmare! You are horrible. That's what you are, horrible!" Then in a fluster of anger she would appoint a staff member to deal with him and hurry away to her resting chamber and wonder if she had been looking

up at the full moon when she conceived hi.
Her own mother had told her it was bad luck
if you did.

During his childhood years Erick also had
an equally bad relationship with his younger
brother, Prince Isaac. It was filled continu-
ously with conflict and rivalry. Erick was
bigger and stronger and could easily subdue
him in any physical challenge, and gloated
victoriously in doing so. Isaac had a flexible,
well-coordinated slender body and could
usually wiggle out of Erick's hold. And he
had an alert fast brain and could often out-
wit his older brother. But sometimes Erick
would have Isaac pinned down solidly, shoving his face in the dirt while twisting his arm
severely. A cruel smile of revenge would play
across his mouth. In these childhood years,
laughter and trust rarely happened between
the two brothers.

According to custom, the day after his sixteenth birthday Erick was turned over to a
chivalrous older knight by the name of Sir
William Ace Chapman, fifty-two. He pre-
ferred to be called Sir Ace and had long been
the king's trusted man, in charge of a very

small royal army whose duty was to protect and defend the kingdom. Sir Ace was highly intelligent, a man of a high warrior class and deeply loyal to the king. He was a very good natural leader who would teach Erick to become a strong knight by using faith, loyalty, honour and, most of all, courage—which Erick seemed to have come by honestly as far as Sir Ace could see. He was the first man Erick had ever met for whom he had instant respect.

In eager compliance Erick sat erect and stationary in his chair and looked expectantly in admiration at his teacher, Sir William Ace Chapman, giving his full attention to the lectures on the history of chivalric warfare and how to master his horsemanship. The teenager was enthralled and instantly became an attentive, obedient student. Later there were lessons in archery and war strategy—the frontal charge, bludgeoning attacks, the value of spreading rumours. Then there was fencing, stick fighting and battlefield swordplay. Erick had never felt like this before. He loved this more than life itself.

Erick's bullying dominance over his

younger brother began to diminish as Isaac grew older, stronger, and more certain of himself. And recently, more often than Erick would admit to himself, a physical challenge between them ended with Isaac as the victor and Erick being forced to admit defeat. He would then withdraw into himself in a brooding and vengeful dark anger.

A few months after Prince Isaac turned sixteen he completed his knighthood studies with high marks Sir Ace noted, but, unlike his brother, he was lacking in genuine enthusiasm. Isaac was a pacifist. He didn't like fighting. He liked it when friends gathered merrily together. Knighthood only interested him when it came to rescuing a damsel in distress.

It was early spring and, by custom, the time for King Thomas to make his annual courtesy visit to the Gypsy village just southwest over the rolling hills of Zymurgy. As far back as memory goes the Kingdom of Zymurgy had always maintained good relations with the Gypsy villagers and their queen. Many of these peace loving people were skilled in arts and crafts. The king decided it was time to take his two sons with him on this visit, time for them to become acquainted with these simple and friendly people. Isaac was eager to go. He liked meeting new people, seeing new sights. Erick grumbled and complained. He had heard peculiar stories about the quaint Gypsy village and their strange inhabitants who dressed in outrageous colours, clung to ancient customs and practiced stupid rituals. Barely above savages, he thought.

Although the short journey would be perfectly safe, the king gave his approval for Sir Ace and two guards to accompany them. More for show than for requirements of the journey, Sir Ace and the guards wore royal uniforms and were armed with swords.

Now, Shway had helped Prince Erick prepare for this journey. Shway had become the prince's devoted servant. He had been dismissed as a royal errand boy, for soon after his father's death he'd become defiant of any authority, used really naughty words to shock the other children of the castle, and had became a bully. Shway had resorted to thievery, had stolen silver and gold from the royals and had pawned many of their belongings. Shway's poor aged mother, who was a chambermaid in service to the queen, pleaded for him to be a good boy but had no control over him whatsoever. The kind king did not torture young Shway for his unruly spiteful crimes. Instead, he'd ordered him into the care of Master David Peek, the royal blacksmith. Shway was to become the lowly helper to the blacksmith, learn the art of the hammer and anvil, sleep in the stable and eat his meals with the servants. He was forbidden to ever enter the formal residence of the palace again.

Shway would often encounter Prince Erick in the stables while he was working on his horse. The prince took a particular liking to Shway as he would do anything the prince asked of him. This elevated Shway's status among the servants and Prince Erick loved having somebody to give orders to, someone who would bow and grovel to him. And today, like so many other days, Shway had helped Prince Erick put on his battle dress, everything except his helmet. To the king's great displeasure Prince Erick insisted on wearing his royal battle garb, with his heavy silver sword strapped to his side. Isaac was weapon free and dressed casually as though left on an island from a shipwreck, except for his shiny black riding boots. This puzzled the king, for Isaac's suave personality and free spirit was unusual.

Just after breakfast they all mounted their horses in the inner courtyard. The morning sun shone down upon them, a cool spring breeze gently played with the large flag that flew high above the castle of Zymurgy. Isaac slipped quickly and easily into the saddle of his horse and couldn't hold back his laughter when Erick had difficulty climbing onto his skittish horse because of his dangling sword. Erick glared hatred at his younger brother. Sir Ace, along with one guard, led the way, signalling for the men to let down the heavy wooden drawbridge. The king and his two sons followed and the other horseman fell in behind as rear guard.

Once outside the castle walls a wide rocky path led them down through the centre of the ancient royal graveyard then onto a worn grass path. A gentle spring breeze blew the long wild grass upon the rolling hills, which led the royal equestrian party southwest. As Sir Ace had precisely navigated, they headed towards the forest and followed an ancient migration trail that took a continuous gentle downward grade, leading them deeper and deeper into a forest filled with giant fir and cedar trees. They then continued on for fifty miles or more towards their destination, where a wondrous mountain and its secluded land were the home of the Gypsy village. There were legends of a magic waterfall and a pond there.

As the six horsemen continued their journey, Isaac remarked on the scenery.

"The topography is stupendous!"

"What are you babbling about, Isaac?" Erick rebuked.

"The topography!…" answered his father. "And if you had been paying closer attention in knighthood training you would understand that your younger brother is referring to the vast spread of trees, the small gullies, the lay of the land. Notice in the distance the few clusters of gigantic ancient fir trees."

Erick slouched and leaned back in his saddle. He hated having his father belittle him in front of the men.

Throughout the forest were brightly coloured birds chirping and darting about. Wild rabbits stood still as the horses passed through, intruding upon their habitat. Colourful sweet-scented spring flowers filled the air and grew plentiful along the edges of the shallow gullies. The air was cool and clean. Spring was surely upon them. Isaac sat comfortably astride his horse, his youthful sixteen-year-old body melding in effortless rhythmic movement with that of his horse. Erick, who was heavier and more solidly built, was having a very unpleasant ride. His horse seemed to be stumbling along and was off rhythm. Also, he was bored with the whole event. Wanting some excitement, and becoming increasingly irritated by the unrelentingly slow plodding of his horse, Erick jabbed his spurs hard in the animal's flanks. He was dying to race wildly through the forest like a madman. The high-strung stallion lurched and sprinted forward ahead of the group a few paces, then stopped abruptly. The king saw the action and frowned with disapproval. Angry with his horse for having stopped, Erick jabbed him again viciously with his spurs. The horse jolted again and tried to throw him off. "Erick!" King Thomas roared angrily.

Sir William Ace Chapman brought his horse forward quickly and grabbed the reins of Erick's horse. "Steady, boy!" he commanded to the horse. This was meant for Erick and the angry young prince knew it. He strained to compose himself. After a moment the procession started out again. Erick turned in his saddle and looked back at his father, his mind racing and his heart pounding like a drum as a dark cloud of hatred moved across his face.

Less than two hours later, as the king and his entourage followed a gentle curve coming in from the northeast, the back of a thousand-foot mountain called Silver Mountain appeared right before their eyes. As they drew nearer they could hear the distant sound of rushing water. They rode farther in towards the base of the mountain, large strange looking roots from ancient fir trees grew upon the granite mountainside like old wrinkled hands holding the weathered rock in place. As the trail continued to curve it took them up a gradual twenty-foot rocky incline, close in, right beside the mountain. Every horse step forward tantalized Isaac's mind as he was amazed by the change in the topography. Finally they reached the west side of the mountain and from its face they could see a beautiful waterfall, its radiant water tumbling down over the rocks.

The horses moved forward at an unhurried pace upon the rocky pathway. There was no need to guide them for a secret path seemed to magically pull them toward a cool misted air that formed by the front of the large waterfall. The cool glistening silver mist from the falls imbued a sense of euphoria in the men as it floated around them, magically evaporating on contact. Isaac sat alert in his saddle, his eyes glistened with excitement, a feast for his senses. Erick hunched forward holding the reins lightly in his left hand, his right hand gripped the handle of his sword tightly as an anxious, suspicious frown twisted his face.

Isaac looked up the rocky mountain face trying to see the source of the falling water, but the uneven grey rock bulged outward and obscured his view. Straight ahead the trail seemed to be heading directly into the falls but then turned left, then right, and then headed in behind the falls. Isaac strained his neck. He couldn't imagine where the water was coming from.

About thirty feet above him the rounded rock structure spread the falling water out into a thin curving sparkling veil, hiding a pond filled with cool water that glistened like silver.

"How is that possible?" Isaac exclaimed to himself. This has to be the magical waterfall and the bottomless pond that his father had told him stories about, with its endless filling of luminous spring water which somehow, mysteriously, came from somewhere inside this small mountain.

"Amazing!" Isaac uttered, straining to look up at the falls.

"This, men, is Slippery Slate Pond," exclaimed the king.

Isaac's heart was pumping fast with excitement. As they went farther along the pathway his mouth fell open and his eyes opened wide in awe for about two hundred feet away, directly in the middle of the trail, was the most gargantuan rotted out ancient evergreen tree stump he had ever seen or could imagine. And out from the top of the tree stump grew beautiful sweet peas of royal purple that hung from a strange green and grey mossy vegetation of vines. Even more sweet peas grew inside and out of the massive structure.

Even after all these years the ancient gigantic sinewy roots were still attached to the rock on the same side of the mountain as the falls. The rest of the exposed roots were held in the hard earth and there the tree miraculously stood, even after hundreds of years of erosion. The most astonishing thing of all was that there was a tunnel; the massive gnarled roots had naturally formed a giant hole right through the middle of the tree. The trail that led into the gaping tunnel seemed to be pulling them, like a magical aura that was inviting them forward. Moving into the dark, Isaac was astonished at how far across it was—wide enough for two horses riding abreast to pass through with plenty of room on the sides. With hardly enough light to see, standing up in his stirrups and reaching up as high as possible, Isaac could just barely touch the mossy vegetation that was growing on the underside of the tunnel. It was soft and left a clean moist smell on his finger tips.

They came out the other side and headed on a downward incline that led to the entrance of the Gypsy Village.

"What are those shiny stones on the ground up ahead of us?" Isaac asked.

King Thomas told them, "The Gypsy people of this village believe that the purple and aqua blue stones scattered on the ground just before the entrance bring good luck to all who enter and leave this village. And the four-foot-high wall over to the left of you goes all the way around this village and partially down by the pond. It was built many many years ago as a protective rock wall, and there is a ledge where you will find imprints of little hands inlaid into it, with the palms facing upward. Each time a new baby is born into this village, an imprint of their hands is added as a sign of peace. They call this *The Wall of Sleeping Palms*, and they are very proud of this monumental work of art."

King Thomas became emotional, tears collected in the corners of his eyes.

Prince Isaac noticed this and was moved by his father's closeness with the people of this village, and hoped that one day he would have the same privilege.

Erick wasn't paying attention and only heard bits and pieces about a wall and that the Gypsies thought it was important, or something of that nature. He was annoyed about having to listen to another lecture and couldn't understand why his father was getting overly emotional.

As he passed over the glass stones Isaac noticed they glistened like magic. And while Erick was impressed by the massive ancient stump and the waterfall, he now looked about the village with disdain and disapproval, seeing only shabbiness. A few Gypsy children ran up to greet them. The king was enormously pleased and Isaac was smiling broadly, waving back happily at the people. A child laughed then threw a flower at Erick, which bounced gently off on to the ground. The haughty young prince turned and looked back at her, then spat on the lucky stones.

Entering the village the men headed straight between two tall fir trees. Hanging ten feet above them from a rope was a hand-carved wooden sign reading, ECAE—Isaac noticed the last letter on the sign was partially weathered off.

Once inside the village there were a few quaint wooden Gypsy caravans spread amongst the trees. The king took his party towards the centre of the village where the Gypsy Queen's caravan stood with others circling a huge firepit.

They were greeted by Tharpe, an extremely handsome and strapping young Gypsy the same age as Prince Erick, who was chopping firewood. He dusted himself off upon seeing them.

The king and his sons got down from their horses. The king introduced Isaac and the others to Tharpe, who always had a few funny stories to tell, then took Erick with him over towards an eerie looking greyish caravan where Arla, the beautiful queen of the village, was pulling strands of silver hair from the head of her daughter, Teaspill. She dropped the strands into a cauldron filled with a strange purple metallic mixture that hung over a slow burning fire, bubbling. They were preparing to make their special Gypsy jewellery from an ancient secret formula.

"I see you are working hard as usual," said the King of Zymurgy.

"Well, look who we have here on this fine first day of spring," Arla said, smiling and giving a slight bow of her head towards the king and his son. "What brings you here so early in the day?"

"I thought I'd like to buy some of your beautiful Gypsy jewellery," King Thomas replied with a wink of his eye.

Erick, who was walking behind his father, was looking at Teaspill. She was the strangest and most lovely girl he had ever laid eyes on.

"This is my oldest son, Erick," said King Thomas, moving his sleek frame aside. Arla turned to look at Erick, her dark eyes widened with fear and distrust. Teaspill turned to look at him too. They both believed the widely spread stories of the bad Prince Erick.

"Good morning, I'm Teaspill. It's nice to

meet you," she said, greeting the oddest looking young man she had ever seen.

"Good morning," Erick said nervously. Mesmerized instantly by her beauty he felt his heart thumping like never before.

"Why don't we go and have a nice cup of purpleberry tea and maybe a little tonic for you, sire," Queen Arla suggested.

"I'll…go for a nice walk with Prince Erick down to the pond," Teaspill said.

The king noticed the young princess was uneasy, then motioned with a wave of his hand and called out for Isaac to go along with them.

The sweet smell of flowers filled the air as the three of them strolled down a pathway lined with blossomed purpleberry bushes. The flowers made Erick's large nose twitch, giving him an idea. He raised his fist to his mouth and let out a huge fake sneeze, then turned towards Isaac, snarled up his top lip, and spoke abruptly.

"I just heard Tharpe calling you back there," lied Erick. He had no use for his younger brother's charming nature and didn't want him along for the walk.

"I dare say it was probably just a lovely bird calling for its mate," Isaac mocked, knowing full well his brother's deceitfulness.

"My father is here to buy some of your jewellery," Erick said to Teaspill.

"How wonderful, it is the strongest and most beautiful jewellery in all the land," the young Gypsy princess informed him.

"Legend has it that your pond is magical," Isaac piped up. "Is this true?"

"Well, yes but…my grandmother told me that it's a secret, and where our jewellery comes from is within our village and nowhere else," Teaspill said.

"What exactly is the jewellery made of?" Isaac asked, puzzled, looking at the silver threads amid her raven black hair.

"Well, I…I'm not really supposed to tell anyone, but seeing you are the king's sons I trust you will keep secret what I tell you," she said.

They took a narrow path that led them to the opening of the ancient old tree stump. They walked inside and the dirt under their feet was moist, smelling like warm earth that had just been rained upon. Their voices echoed within the dark space as they made light conversation about the village. Teaspill led the way and walked between Erick and Isaac, she knew the path like the beat of her own heart. As they walked, Erick reached out his hand and quickly stroked the back of Teaspill's hair in a downward motion. A chill ran from where he touched her head and tingled right down her spine. She quickly reached back to feel if something had fallen from the ancient trees roots onto her hair, but nothing had.

Suddenly, in a reprimanding deceptive tone of voice, Erick spoke sharply towards his younger brother.

"Isaac, didn't our mother teach you to keep your hands to yourself? I'm sure the princess may now think poorly of you. I apologize for my brother's ignorance."

Isaac held his tongue as his envious brother challenged him once again.

Coming through to the other side of the hollow stump there were giant gnarled exposed roots that had even crawled out from under the ground inside the old tree stump, and from where they stood, looking down ten feet, one could see a large slippery slate of rock that sloped downward into the endless glistening fresh clean water of the pond.

"We can sit here and rest and I will tell you a little about the magic of our village," Teaspill said in a soft voice. Erick plunked himself down first. Isaac waited like a gentlemen and motioned with his hand for Teaspill to sit upon one of the big roots. Before Isaac sat he noticed some pretty purple sweet peas growing up between the gnarled roots so he reached down, picked one, and gently gave it to Teaspill.

"Oh, for me?" she said. "Why thank you, how very sweet of you, Prince Isaac." She tucked it in her black and silver hair, above her ear.

"You're very welcome," Isaac said, sitting on a root closer to her than Erick. After all it's not every day a prince gets to spend time with a Gypsy princess as lovely as yourself," he added.

"And, it's not every day that a man such as yourself is brave enough to touch the mystifying hair of the Gypsy princess," Teaspill concluded.

Erick seethed with jealousy, he wanted to punch his brother out cold. But for some strange reason Teaspill's loveliness drew both Erick and Isaac into a deep trance. Just hearing her soft voice made them both stare into her glimmering mystical eyes as she began to tell the secret story.

"My mother, our Gypsy queen, wears the magical heirloom locket necklace," she said in a whisper.

Hearing her soft voice Erick was suddenly hypnotized, his brain went all fuzzy. He could hardly hear her voice, his heart was beating beyond excitement. Her hair of black shone with silver threads and caught the rays of sunlight reflecting off the pond, her lips had an inviting silver sparkle upon them. As bold as it seemed, he imagined kissing her dainty lips. Not hearing a word of her story and with his eyes now closed, he leaned toward her, puckering his dry skinny lips for a romantic kiss. Teaspill cocked her neck back, shocked and embarrassed. Isaac was listening attentively but had become distracted while watching his lovestruck brother make a complete fool of himself and had to bite his cheek to keep from dying of laughter. All of a sudden Erick's eyes popped open wide, disoriented, his hands flew from his lap and grabbed each side of the big root he sat upon to gain his sense of balance. Teaspill stood up, uncertainty crawled throughout her whole being.

"Well, this has been a…an…unusual visit!" Teaspill exclaimed.

Erick, still not fully out of his spellbound love fantasy, felt that his gallant brother had hampered his moment and ruined Princess Teaspill's first impression of him.

"Ah…yes…," stated Erick, lightheaded, the blood pulsating in his temples.

Prince Isaac thanked Teaspill. Keeping her distance from Prince Erick, Teaspill quickly led the way back through the big hollow stump and hoped that she would never see Prince Erick again. Isaac felt terrible and was embarrassed of his brother. Erick assumed that, being the future King of Zymurgy, he would one day soon have another opportunity to woo Teaspill.

The three of them walked back toward the centre of the village, speaking uncomfortably in turn.

When they returned the king had just finished his visit with Queen Arla and had bought some lovely jewellery to take back with him. They said their goodbyes and headed back to the castle of Zymurgy.

On the way home, Isaac, being a very impressionable young lad, bragged like an overwound music box about all the great things he had seen and done that day. The king listened attentively. Erick's imagination could only conjure up ideas of how, when he became king, he would make his better look-ing brother a failing court jester. He would then have the right to chop his brother's head off instead of having to plan another way to get rid of him.

When they arrived back at the castle it was already getting dark. The king, Erick and Isaac guided their horses to the stables. The King dismounted and spoke to the sta-ble master. A few stalls away Erick and Isaac had also dismounted and turned their horses over to the stable assistants.

"I enjoyed myself immensely today," said Isaac, and added, "Did you happen to take notice of the beautiful artwork on the stained glass locket necklace that Queen Arla was wearing around her neck? Such an incredible village of humble hardworking people."

"You know Erick, Teaspill thinks I'm rather sweet," he taunted.

"Well…I'm going back, to ask for her hand in marriage!" Erick declared. "And what do you think of that?"

"Well, from what I understand from our visit today, you're…not her type," Isaac informed him. Isaac glanced at Erick and slowly slid his hand down his puffed out chest.

"Teaspill's mine! She should be so lucky to marry someone like me—an heir to the throne," Erick boasted.

Isaac roared with laughter at the statement his brother had made, knowing full well that Teaspill found him rude and disgusting. "You're a fool," Isaac said, laughing even harder.

The conflict caught the attention of the king.

Erick had become filled with a powerful dark emotion that was gathering force rapidly. "You find that funny, do you," he challenged in a loud voice. The two were standing by an empty stall, close to where Isaac's horse was kept, when Erick drew his sword from its sheath.

"Now, now, calm down dear brother," Isaac mocked, noticing that his brother had become irate with his taunting.

"Draw your sword!" Erick demanded.

Isaac stood fearfully without a sword and held his arms up to surrender, remembering that his father had taught him a knight should only use his sword in a life or death situation. Perhaps that might be now, he thought.

With murderous intent, Erick viciously thrust his sword at his brother's heart. Isaac ducked but the lethal weapon ripped deeply into his shoulder. He cried and fell to the ground in pain while Erick ripped the bowed sword from his brother's flesh.

"You are the weakest of all, you little baby of daddy's!" Erick gasped in dripping envy.

Isaac writhed on the ground, bleeding and in shock, not understanding how his own flesh and blood could be so brutal.

Seeing with his own eyes what had been done, devastation struck the king's heart.

"Retreat," King Thomas bellowed.

Erick moved away from Isaac and threw his sword onto the stable floor, then he stood still as his father approached them swiftly.

"Your mother was right! You are a HORRIBLE man," King Thomas roared, leaving the barn with Isaac, then ordering two nearby royal guards to seize Erick and take him to a holding cell in a tower at the rear of the castle until His Royal Highness made a serious decision. This would affect his whole family and the kingdom around them. Later that evening King Thomas collapsed to his knees, he cried in heart-wrenching pain to the world and to his wife, for he felt he had somehow failed his son. Asking Sir Ace Chapman to bring him the caged black dove of ill fate, the king put the dark bird to flight to deliver the most embarrassing letter he had ever sent, requesting his dear old friend Lord Gibor Barbcott—the oldest and wisest judge in the land—to come right away to the castle of Zymurgy.

That next morning Erick awoke from a restless sleep where he lay on a hard rock floor, was still chained and with the same wrinkled clothes on as the day before. Hearing the sound of a squeaky old carriage entering the courtyard and the drawbridge chain being pulled up, he crawled to his feet and went to the window where he saw Lord Barbcott arriving in his ancient crimson and black horse-drawn carriage. Greeted by King Thomas and Queen Catherine, he stepped out of the carriage, removed his fancy crystal top hat, and bowed to the royal couple. Erick noticed he was wearing the long royal red-hooded judge's cloak with its dreaded plum sash and solid gold pin depicting a setting sun pierced through by a knight's sword. Erick knew he was in serious trouble.

By the next morning a series of meetings amongst family and noble men were finally finished—a decision had been made.

Two large royal guards dressed in formal uniforms unlocked Erick's cell in the dingy tower. With his hands and feet still chained, they led him down a narrow winding rock stairwell through the darkness in the back part of the castle. Finally, reaching ground level, they came out through a secret door that led them into a dark hallway where a couple of young maidservants were sneaking about. One knew where they had put Erick, the other fancied the prince and she stepped forward to give him a drink from a golden goblet, but one of the big guards slapped it to the ground so the two woman ran off afraid.

Struggling with the guards, Erick was taken down another stairwell into an area where thick stone walls supported several underground dungeons, then he was taken past a huge heavy iron gate. Up above the gate and the dungeons was where the ancient Court of Zymurgy stood. Beside the courthouse was a mournful garden not prepared for spring. In a corner of this garden stood a beautiful statue of a damsel bride with her golden knight on bent knee looking up at her, his helmet cradled in his arm and his sword by his side. This statue was called, *Noble Knight of Zymurgy*. Usually a wreath of fresh flowers sat upon the bride's head but, today, in sadness, the statue would be covered with a black smock, for this was the first time in history that a prince would be tried in the great court of Zymurgy.

Back down under the ancient courtroom, Erick protested.

"Let go of me!" he demanded. "Don't

touch me. Unhand me at once you peasants. I'm your future king! Let…go…of me!" And they did. The guards finally threw him into a bat-ridden cell with walls of stone that were fifteen feet high and round like a well. Up above him on the peak of a cone-shaped ceiling was an opening the size of a dinner plate for light to come in. As the big wooden cell door slammed shut, Erick put his head against the cold stone wall and kicked it. While he waited for his trial to come to session he looked around and saw a skinny old rat with its beady eyes aglow, it was finishing off the remains of a dead bat. It looked at him then escaped through a hole in the wall.

Erick was livid and wished he were the rat and thought how a good lie might help him out. He moved about nervously inside the dark, cold, claustrophobic cell waiting for the crowd of spectators, council and jury to take their places above him in the courtroom. From under the door he could hear the humming of low voices as people chatted in the hallway, their feet scuffling across the cobblestones like sandpaper on clay. Erick's attention was drawn quickly to the cell door as he heard a familiar voice outside. It was Shway, who had, over the years, remained the disdainful prince's devoted servant.

"Master!" yelled Shway, stopping with the two maidens that Erick had seen earlier.

The massive guard standing outside the cell door looked down his nose at the three of them and ordered them to move on.

Inside the courtroom ten noble knights had already taken their seats in the jury box, one of them being Sir Ace Chapmen, along with five other well-established citizens of Zymurgy. This was a special open court day and the huge gold painted wooden doors of the beautiful ancient Court House of Zymurgy were opened wide. There were ten big royal guards dressed in black and gold Zymurgy courtroom attire; two of them stood at the front door of the courthouse to guide the people inside. So many came from near and far that they couldn't all fit into the courtroom. Other guards directed the rest of the excited crowd over to the royal jousting field where they sat in the stands and looked down into a large enclosed area where six court jesters ran around in brightly coloured satin costumes performing strange panto-mimes, juggling and chasing fat pigs around while throwing them stale bread and succu-lent fruit to fatten them up. Later in the eve-ning the pigs would be roasted and feasted upon by the people in the palace, to celebrate the absence of evil.

Now, back below the courthouse, in the dark guts of the dungeon, two large guards opened the creaky door of Erick's cell and escorted him to another door where a secret solid gold staircase led them up through a pri-vate open hatch entrance into the courtroom. After chaining Erick to a heavy weight that was situated on a round wooden platform on the floor, they closed the hatch and two guards stood on either side of him. Prince Erick held his head high in arrogance. Everyone looked at him. Then, three trumpets sounded to indicate that the king and queen were about to make their entrance onto a private court-house balcony looking down over the peo-ple inside. They sadly took their places upon their thrones while the large crowd stood and bowed, paying their respects.

Erick seethed with anger and glared at his

mother and father. In his mind he justified what he had done to his younger brother. Seeing Isaac, Erick stabbed him with a stare of vengeance and knew that one day he'd make them all pay for what they were doing to him. Prince Isaac looked away with tears in his eyes and wished none of this had ever happened.

A noble clergyman stepped forward, announcing that the proceedings were to begin.

A fragile-looking, very old Gibor Barbcott—wearing his crystal top hat, royal red robe and plum sash with the sparkly gold pin upon it—shuffled his way out through a velvet curtain onto a smaller balcony just beside the king and the queen. He removed his hat with the oval mirror that crested the front and put it aside. He bowed to the royal couple then turned his stiff neck and stared down at Erick, speaking very clearly in a painfully slow manner.

"Raise…your…right…hand," he drawled, holding up the Book of Knights which ruled the land of Zymurgy. He proceeded through the rest. "How…do you plead?"

"INNOCENT!" Erick bellowed.

"GUILTY!" Gibor Barbcott yelled loudly

to Erick, shocking the people in the court-room. Even the crowd outside heard him yell, and the king and queen jumped in their seats. Then Barbcott stated calmly, "It has been agreed upon by everyone, wherever they may be." No one ever disagreed with old Lord Barbcott. The crowd stayed still.

"Next!" stated Barbcott. "Prince… Isaac… take the royal chair… would you please."

Isaac was tense as he approached the big chair and stood in front of it, taking the knight's oath of honesty. He then sat and told the whole truth about the ordeal, before returning to where he'd been sitting earlier with two big guards.

The jury watched him closely. Old Barb-cott looked around then made his decision.

"By a pardon from your… mother… a town called Petalville will become yours, and now Prince Erick… you… will be given a… new name. It shall be… a horrible name. It will be agh… Horrible Horribin. Your title… The Tainted Knight. And you will be banished from the mighty castle of Zymurgy, never to set foot on this land again."

Then Erick was escorted outside into the

crowd of people by two big guards and taken down to the jousting field where the court jesters ran off, afraid when they saw a coffin arriving. Everyone had left the courthouse and gone to sit around the jousting field.

Erick hated his new title and thought if they were going to call him that, he was going to live up to it. Then, looking about, he noticed the Knights of Zymurgy's small army parading on their horses out of an archway from the stables behind the jousting field walls. Passing by him, they gathered by a large open metal coffin that sat on a flatbed carriage in the centre of the field. It had been brought out earlier by two big horses and a guard who still stood beside the large lid, which had been placed on the ground. The Knights of Zymurgy were gallantly dressed in dark golden ceremonial armour. They were wearing a special kind of helmet made of solid gold, called, *The Helmet of the Setting Sun*. Sad but beautiful, this headpiece, with its sharp short spikes, resembled a setting sun. It was pierced by an ornamental gold sword, indicating that the sun was never again going to rise or set upon the lustrous armour of the Tainted Knight, Erick. The royal headpiece was only worn when a crime was committed by a knight belonging to the royal family.

Dark grey clouds gathered low in the sky as though a storm was coming. The noble knights had now formed a straight line side by side; then, a large beautiful brown horse appeared from a grander archway and galloped out from between heavy open iron gates. As it came across the field, its hooves raised the dry dirt to dust. Riding high upon the mighty animal was a huge knight adorned in a magnificent rich blood-red suit of armour. He stopped in the centre of the field where Prince Erick's suit of armour was being displayed in a coffin filled with a shiny liquid, for everyone to see.

Now Erick, who was standing back a way with the two guards, wondered what was going on. As he couldn't see what was inside the coffin from where he stood, he focused on the scary sight of it and became frightened. "Are they going to kill me?" he thought to himself. He struggled as the guards brought him right up in front of the carriage and made him climb a short set of wooden stairs so he could look into the coffin. At first all he could see was his own miserable angry face in the reflection of a strange smelling chemical liquid. Then, as he looked deeper, he saw his most beautiful possession—the shiny suit of armour that his father had given him for his sixteenth birthday. Erick began to tremble, while the crowd seemed silent. He seethed with dark anger as he turned and jumped down from the stairs, twisting and pulling the two guards to the ground with him. Getting up, the guards grabbed him by the chains on his arms and made him stand still. Then one of the noble Knights of Zymurgy that was lined up with the others came forward upon his horse. He was holding a scroll which he unrolled and read as an announcement.

By order of King Thomas and Queen
Catherine Horribin of Zymurgy,
this once obedient and honourable knight's suit,
given as a gift of nobility to Prince Erick
Cornelius Horribin,
shall steep in this box and slowly corrode away

like the opportune teachings that he denied himself.
And it shall be hidden beneath the dungeon floors of this castle forever.

The crowd gasped in horror, some booed Prince Erick, some cried. Erick's knighthood brothers sat still upon their horses. A knight with a burning torch cantered forward then galloped around the coffin once, holding the torch high into the air. Then he dismounted to help the guard lift the heavy lid and place it back on top of the coffin. The two bowed to the king and queen who, along with Lord Barbcott and Isaac, were sitting up in the royal jousting balcony.

The knights all galloped around the field once, then rode back through the archway to the stables once more.

As the crowd calmed down they started to leave, for the day had been long.

A single guard slowly led the two horses with the carriage and the heavy coffin with the steeping royal suite of armour swishing and swaying about inside it, some of the liquid spilling out and sizzling as it hit the ground. The carriage finally reached the shadows of the castle's open metal gates and disappeared, to be hidden in a secret place forever.

Erick watched the coffin as it was taken away and noticed it dripped from one side. He figured there may be a leak somewhere. He turned around and swallowed hard knowing that there was but one large knight left sitting upon his horse, pointing straight at him.

Not to be messed with and not wearing The Helmet of the Setting Sun, but a blood-red helmet and suit of armour, was Sir William Ace Chapman. He removed his heavy helmet and looked down at Erick. Great disappointment crossed his aged face. Erick held his ground and remained in control of his feelings, although if anyone had ever made him feel weak it was Sir Ace Chapman. Nevertheless, Erick remained strong. Ace remained silent and looked at Prince Erick, trying to find a glimmer of what used to be. Nobly putting his helmet back on as it hid the emotions he still had for the young prince, he turned his horse and rode back toward the big gates and into the castle wondering what had happened to this young man.

Everyone had gone except Shway, who was frightened to death. He sat crying, not knowing what they were going to do with his master. Shway went into protective mode, knowing that something really awful was about to happen. He needed to sneak about. It was dangerous to follow Prince Erick at this time but Shway was determined to help his master. Shway thought of a plan. He would find out what they were going to do with Erick. Shway wiped his eyes with his sweaty hands and recovered from his crying stint. He saw Prince Erick walking towards the stables in cuffs and rattling chains that clanged around his wrists and ankles, struggling all the way, not speaking to the guards. He was almost free and tried to control his anger. He would kill his brother if he could get his hands on him.

The king and queen had been watching from a high balcony as their son was taken away to the stables to be abolished. The king rose, looking disgusted in his son for showing no remorse for his younger brother, and the queen also rose, with tears in her eyes, her head shaking in anger and embarrassment. All the long years with this horrible young man had finally come to an end and now the castle would be free of the pain and suffering that they'd lived with for so many years. Yet it would seem so strange without him.

Princess Remoh had been spared the anguish of this event and had spent a lovely day with Annette in a remote part of the castle playing games, having tea and learning to play her piano, which was more settling than this disgusting event.

Isaac, who had gone back inside the castle, had many guards around him for protection. He never understood his brother's hatred towards him or how he could have turned so viciously on his own blood. Now Isaac would always be looking over his shoulder for fear that one day Erick may try to kill him because, one day, Isaac would be the king.

Meanwhile, Erick was escorted by two guards into the stables. They were instructed to keep a close hand on him, to keep him chained and give him no weapons.

Soon after that Shway had crept his way

into the stables and overheard two guards discussing Prince Erick and how he was going to be taken away that very same day. Young Shway hurried off fretfully. He gathered some of his belongings, stole some food, and disguised himself as a common civilian leaving the castle grounds on horseback by way of the open drawbridge doors, along with some other stragglers that were leaving the courtyard from the event earlier that day. Shway rode his horse far out beyond the castle walls and waited, hidden amongst the trees, until he saw four guards take Prince Erick north of the castle. Shway secretly followed them. They rode far into the forest and up into the mountains with Horrible chained to his horse. After many hours of travelling the guards finally released Erick and he bolted off into the forest, kicking his horse hard in the girth. Screaming like a madman, he exclaimed,

"You'll all pay for this one day!"

Prince Erick was banished forever for his behaviour would have disgraced his family's name. Shway caught up with Horrible and they journeyed all over, creating a rebellious life together. Horrible had been cast out and was an angry bitter young man who knew that his brother would now become heir to the throne, and he would be renowned throughout the kingdom as Horrible Horribin—The Tainted Knight.

Queen Arla had learned of the brazen advances towards her daughter when Erick had visited the Gypsy village. She was alarmed and told the king of her concern.

Because of Horrible's bad reputation throughout the lands, Teaspill's mother issued an edict that would prevent him from entering their village ever again.

As in years before, the present royal Gypsy family guarded their queen and kept her safe, along with the magical secret of their family heirloom—the stained glass locket necklace they called, the *Knight of Wishhearts.*

THREE

❧⚮❧

ECAE

Many, many years later, on a crisp fall morning, a cool wind swayed the old wooden village sign that hung over the entrance to the Gypsy village. The last letter had still not been fixed and was now worn right off; it seems it had taken a terrible beating over the years. The good luck stones of purple and aqua were now covered by crunchy frost-ridden leaves which whirled around and around as the wind troubled them. Still nestled amongst the trees were the Gypsies caravans. A subtle frost had given the brightly decorated homes on wheels a sugar-coated appearance, and they sparkled in the sunshine. Larger caravans of the village encircled a big community firepit where children were frolicking about with their games and the men and women were occupied with their chores.

The big firepit was where the Gypsy families gathered together for all sorts of occasions. Each family had their own bench made of large hollowed out tree trunks.

The trees were sparkling with frost, the sun was shining through the branches and everyone in the village was excited, for tomorrow was the most exciting day of the year, Ecae day, the day the village was named after. Everyone was hustling and bustling and preparing for what needed to be done.

A few of the Gypsy children were picking berries from the purpleberry bushes for the delicious berry pies. They hid behind the bushes when they saw Footmeyer hobbling swiftly down the pathway toward them. Their eyes sparkled as they wiped their little stained lips before Footmeyer could catch them popping the star-shaped berries into their mouths.

Charlie Footmeyer Woods was his real name but everyone called him Footmeyer. He looked like a mad possum with his beady little translucent blue eyes seemingly glued into the corners of his short pointy nose. His coarse salt and pepper hair was braided into a ponytail and hung down his back to meet the overalls that wrapped the thick trunk of his body like a pear skin. The pant legs of his overalls were rolled up at the bottom, his right leg missing from the knee down and replaced by a peg of wood. The same old story about how he lost it never changed. The children would listen attentively, their eyes growing wider and wider as they heard the story of how it happened. Footmeyer would squint his beady possum eyes, as he told it.

"One day I accidentally slipped into a deep mucky mud puddle and when I tried to pull my leg out half of it was gone, never to be seen again."

Looking down at the faces of the puzzled children, Footmeyer would shake his wide head and shrug his hunched shoulders, then he would reach into his pocket and take out an old rag and wipe the sweat from his furrowed brow as though he had fought a great battle. The story usually came when he needed a rest.

"How can we have a celebration with the last letter of the village entrance sign missing?" he yelled. Footmeyer always yelled.

He noticed the children's little purple stained mouths, a faint smirk twisted the corners of his mouth. He loved the small troubles they caused him.

"Tisk, tisk," Footmeyer said, "hmm … purple lips? You all look sick and can't possibly come to the celebration tomorrow. I'll tell your mothers to put you all to bed," he winked at them. They laughed at him as he headed back towards the centre of the village.

Footmeyer ran the village. Inside that big head of his all was organized. He had specific plans, a list of things to do to make sure everything ran smoothly for tomorrow.

Gypsy time had rolled along and now, being mid-afternoon, it seemed on this lovely autumn day that there was someone else in this village making a list, a list of bad things to do. It was Horrible Horribin, who at this time in his unrewarding life had become a bitter, sinister old man. By his side was his faithful, absent-minded accomplice Shway, who had kept his promise and reunited with his master. The two men had snuck their way into the peaceful Gypsy village through a crumbled part of the back wall. At this moment they were perched high up in the top of a big tree, camouflaged in cheesy costumes that Shway had made by sewing real autumn leaves to their clothing, and they were spying on the Gypsies. Now Horrible Horribin had become a skinny wretched codger of a man with a huge nose and crooked rotten teeth. His offensive personality had developed into that of a mad dog. He held a spyglass in one bony hand and his sword-handled cane in the other. His white and grey prickly eyebrows slithered back to join his slick white porcupine hair.

Shway had grown into a giant simpleton who couldn't read or write. He moved awkwardly as though his long legs were made of wooden stilts. Some years before he had lost one of his ears in battle and his thin stringy-looking hair was greasily plastered to his narrow skull.

"Look at them, Shway," snarled Horrible, looking disgusted as he crouched in the tree, glaring down at the people in the village with hatred in his eyes.

Shway didn't hear him as his one ear was missing and he wasn't paying attention, instead he was watching the children of the village run around and play. He sighed, wishing that he too could be like them.

Horrible poked him in the ribs with his cane to get his attention. Shway turned to look at him. He was hideously dressed up in his fall leaf attire to camouflage their dastardly scheme.

Shway could hardly contain his laughter. "I like your bonnet," he said politely. The array of leaves that encircled Horrible's head added a special touch to his leafy suit and cold waxy red nose.

"What are you looking at?" Horrible sneered in a whisper.

"You look funny," said Shway with a dunce laugh, as he stuffed his large fist into his horse teeth.

"Ha, ha, ha...you made it!" said Horrible in a demeaning fashion.

"Yes, sir," answered Shway, holding in his girly giggles.

"Why, you're a sight to behold," Horrible retorted with his head cocked back.

"Thank you," replied Shway, tipping his head in honour.

"You are a big leafless lumpus!" Horrible said, spitting through his teeth.

"Lumpus?" Shway repeated Horrible's last word, rolling his eyes up into his head and trying very hard to understand its meaning.

"Stop this ridiculousness at once!" Horrible snapped. "We have a job to do!"

"Why are we up so ha…high in this tree?" Shway said, feeling faint. "Wh…wh…what are we s'pose to be doin' again?"

"We're…here…to destroy this village and steal the locket necklace. The heirloom!…You lumpus idiot." Horrible clenched his teeth then poked Shway hard in the ribs once again with the sharp handle of his cane. Bringing his odd looking spyglass back up to one of his evil eyes to take a look down into the village, he was met with Shway's large magnified face. "You're in my way," he snapped. Then, in an conspiratorial whisper, he explained his despicable scheme.

"Every year these crazy Gypsies carry on with this petty little celebration, a waste of time. I need to get that heirloom locket from the old Gypsy woman, even if I have to ki—!"

Horrible stopped. "Err...I need to put an end to this ridiculous event," he grumbled.

"Kiss her for it," Shway responded, batting his eyelashes.

Horrible turned and glared at Shway, his angry eyes were pierced with fire.

Meanwhile Footmeyer had stopped at the village baker. "Good afternoon, Golly," he yelled.

Golly Sweetman was the sweetest man of the caravans, as round as his rolls. He was wearing his large purple patched work apron and puffy baker's hat, he sang and rocked his rotund belly from side to side, a jolly fellow he was.

"I have pies and cakes, goodies and dates," he sang. "Sweet chocolate hands and cinnamon strands. Everything is ready to go, for I am the sweetest man you'll ever know."

"By Golly, you are the sweetest man I know," yelled Footmeyer, doing a little swayzee butts dance. His polka-dotted undershorts flopped out from a rip in his overalls as he swung his rear end and hopped in double time over to Miss Tressy's caravan. Tressy was the best hair dresser in all the village and ran the Hairavan.

"Hi there, Miss Tressy," yelled Footmeyer, keeping his distance.

"Hi, Footmeyer," yelled Tressy.

Tressy's hair was rolled up in warm tin cans and wrapped with old woollen work socks around her tiny head. Tressy could yell almost as loud as Footmeyer and he often thought if anything were to happen to him, she could take over his job. Footmeyer had his reasons for keeping his distance.

Miss Tressy experimented with the village people's hair and she was a crazy sight herself. She resembled a waif. Her fire red hair stuck out from the ends of the tin cans as though a high voltage electrical charge had taken over her head. A ragged shawl barely covered her frail shoulders and her skinny legs, much like a sparrow's, didn't look like they could hold her up. Her first victims, the twins, left her Hairavan parlour with their hair braided in the middle—binding them together—and each had a braid on either side. The father of the twins wore a brand new toupee made from the hair of Tressy's horse's tail. It had been made for this special occasion and was glued tightly to his head. He and the twins thanked her and quickly left, as Tressy wore a foul-smelling poultice of strong potent spices in a cheesecloth wrapped around her neck, a secret family custom that had been passed down for centuries by her ancestors. The smell made everyone gag, but it kept her from getting sick in the cold winter months. She made like it didn't bother her.

Footmeyer tried to stand downwind as the smell of Tressy's poultice wafted through the air.

"Want your hair cut too?" Tressy yelled.

Footmeyer hurried away. "Nice work, see you tomorrow," he called from a distance.

"Okay," screamed Tressy, as she helped her next victim, a poor little boy, get up onto a sawed off, wobbly, three-foot-high upright log used as a hairdressing stool. She told the boy how Footmeyer's braid was one day going to grow so long it would trip him and he would break his wooden leg. The child just held his nose peg in place as Tressy's poultice was so stinky. It was unavoidable, with the crisp breeze whipping the scent around the village.

Footmeyer finally approached his own

artistically painted caravan. His wife, Soaprah, called it the Perfumavan. From it came the most beautiful aroma in all the village. Soaprah was a tall big-boned woman, so large in size that Footmeyer had to make the door frame of the Perfumavan larger so she could fit through it. Her disposition was as delightful as the sweet peas that were still holding their own against the early frost. Her heavy-set arms and legs moved slowly about as she prepared for the big celebration. Soaprah's big soft brown eyes and crooked grin brought much happiness to the people of the village. She had made delicate scarves, lavender sachets, purpleberry soap, and lip dips from sweet tree sap. Soaprah loved this time of year for this Ecae day was going to be extra special. She had made a beautiful purple scarf for Isa, the new Gypsy queen to be, and a striking purple patchwork quilt for her first grandchild, who would soon be born.

Soaprah primped at the beautiful crocheted cap she had made. It hugged her completely bald head. She caught a glance of Footmeyer coming down the path towards her.

"Vud you like some purpleberry tonic?"

she asked, batting her long soft black eyelashes and winking sweetly at him.

"I will get some tomorrow," Footmeyer called out, as he passed by the sweet peas hanging from the arched garden gate of the Perfumavan's entrance.

"Good afternoon, my dear," he added as he hurried on, pretending not to notice his wife's little gestures of love. He knew she would be ready for tomorrow with her gifts of love and peace for all to enjoy.

Gypsy time was moving along, this was different from most time. Hans, a big partially dug out log, stood vertically on end not far from Tressy's Hairavan. He was built many years ago so the village people had a way of telling time. As a matter of fact, Hans had no hands, but he did have Bing and Bong, two very small muscular hairy Gypsy brothers with short strong arms and legs. How they loved to sing jingles and today's went like this.

My name is Bing, my name is Bong,
we cling and clang all day long.
It's quite absurd, as our sound disturbs

the village if you may.
The time when told, is loud and bold,
but precise every time.
And Hans, the clock, he's got no tick-tock,
just Bing and Bong's symbols that never stop.

And so they would climb inside the hollowed out log, Bing right side up and Bong upside down. Strapped to their heads were shiny metallic symbols, inside their ears were plugs. Every hour on the hour they would push with their bare feet from the inside ends of the log towards each other, causing the symbols to clang together loudly. Then they would jump out and proudly exchange upside down handshakes and bow towards each other for an extra clang. After that they would hurry over to sit and rest on a nearby log until it was time to do this again.

It was almost evening now and Horrible and Shway were still lurking up in the tree tops. They needed to get down and begin their awful evil plan, for evening was soon to come.

"I'm getting cold. Can we please get down now?" asked Shway in a pleading tone.

"No, you can't," snapped Horrible. "I mean, yes," he added in a sickly sweet way.

"After you," said Horrible, as he motioned Shway to shimmy down the tree. Horrible followed him. "Now, ah-hem," ordered Horrible abruptly, "your job is to hand out these goodies to all the little Gypsy children." He reached in his pocket for the prepared packets.

Shway wiggled with excitement, hopping up and down.

"What are the goodies?"

"They're not for you!" Horrible yelled at him. Then the deposed prince composed himself. "They're special little bags of pretty sparkling fire dust. You're going to be a big part of this celebration, Shway. Now, hand these out to the children and tell them to sprinkle the pretty dust all around their village, especially on the caravans wheels," he emphasized.

Shway had never seen Horrible look so horrible but he did what he was told and tricked all the sweet innocent children while the wicked wretched Horrible Horribin peered through his spyglass from behind the purpleberry bushes to make sure Shway didn't miss one single child. Shway snuck around so as not to be seen by any grownups. When Shway was finished he scrambled back into the bushes and assured Horrible that he had given out all of the little presents which would make the Gypsy celebration an even more special event than ever before. Shway then laughed like the dunce he was.

Horrible and Shway made their way back out through a broken piece in the village wall where they had camouflaged their horses and the funny-looking rickety metal cart, which Shway had built to transport their suits of armour, swords and heavy Morning Star flails that they were going to use to destroy the village wall.

"Now, we wait," said Horrible with a sinister look, as he crouched low in the bushes.

"Wait for who?" asked Shway in a loud whisper.

"We wait…for the right time, you idiot!" growled Horrible.

"Yes, sir," spouted Shway.

Horrible covered Shway's mouth roughly with the leafy arm of his shirt sleeve.

"Get out our equipment, Shway," Horrible demanded. "It's time to dress in honour of me." Shway opened the cart doors and gave Horrible the pieces of his heavy knight suit to put on, then clumsily put on his own. He then reached into the cart and brought out two big Morning Star flails and excitedly laid them on the ground.

"Now...hand me my big sword, Shway," Horrible commanded.

Shway looked down into the cart, leaned far into the opening of it and stuck his long gangly arms inside. Feeling around, he was shocked to find no sword. With a stiff neck he raised his head then turned and grinned sheepishly at Horrible, pretending that he was going to bring out Horrible's big sword any minute now.

"My sword!" Horrible demanded.

Horrible held out his cane in exchange for his prize possession sword. Shway looked at him out of the corners of his eyes, then he reached into the cart once more and pulled out his stuffed teddy bear and clung on to it tightly. He'd remembered his prize possession.

"You...idiot, where...is...my...sword," Horrible growled.

Horrible let his spyglass drop—it hung from a rusty chain around his neck—then he grabbed Shway's teddy bear, stuck it on the end of his cane and hurled it high up into the trees. Down it fell, branch by branch, until it flopped onto the ground. Shway's bottom lip dropped, then quivered in despair. He crossed his arms, closed his eyes, and turned childishly away from Horrible, not wanting to play anymore. Unknowingly the two villains had hidden closer to the village than they'd thought, for the joyous laugher of a child filled the air as, through the thickets, Shway's sad eyes spotted a small Gypsy boy. He had picked up Shway's teddy bear, hugged it, and skipped away. Shway turned towards Horrible with a wide mouth grin. He felt he had somehow defeated him.

"How am I suppose to win the battle with a cane? You fool!" growled Horrible through his gritted teeth. He shook his cane wildly towards Shway, who's eyes bugged out.

The two villains stayed hidden and now

had to wait for sundown to come to the humble Gypsy village. They're evil plan was perfectly intact.

Meanwhile, Footmeyer was finishing his chores for the day. He wondered if King Isaac was going to join them for their celebration tomorrow. He often went hunting in the woods and would come to visit Garth, Footmeyer's son. Garth was an unusually handsome young man, his ancestry was of ancient royal Gypsy blood. He had broad shoulders and was strong as an ox. His light brown curly hair hung down over his shoulders and he had the blue, almond-shaped eyes of a wolf. His temperament was like his mother Soaprah—calm and protective. He was talented and worked alongside his father. They made hand-crafted stained glass windows for the Gypsy caravans and beautiful water fountains for the courtyards of the castles across the lands.

The sun was slowly sinking and Footmeyer was getting tired so he sat down on one of the family logs. Usually around this time of day his one good foot would need a rest. As he looked up into the trees he admired their majestic form. Just a few more things to do he thought to himself, then noticed the children running around skipping and laughing. They had sprinkled sparkly dust around the grounds, he supposed Soaprah had given it to them to play with.

Soaprah and Footmeyer were both born here in the village and had spent their whole lives together. Just a year ago their son Garth married Madam Teaspill's beautiful daughter, Princess Isa. Isa had shiny black hair with hints of silver threads. Her skin was delicate like a white rose, her eyes were of soft grey and silver. Her personality was mesmerizing, yet gentle like a new fawn. Her slight body was covered with a long delicate purple cotton dress. Over her dress was a black hooded cape and on her small feet were dark grey leather boots. Isa was agile yet displayed the strength of a young boy.

This beautiful young girl was to become the new Gypsy queen of the village tomorrow, on Ecae day, and inherit the family heirloom from her aging mother, Madam Teaspill. Isa was also going to receive another gift, she was heavy with child and any day now would become a mother. Lately she was often found resting in her caravan.

Footmeyer was excitedly impatient for his new grandchild to arrive, his very own little purpleberry picking child. Footmeyer's daydreaming was getting in the way of his chores once again. As he sat on a log bench resting, he pulled off his one big rubber boot, turned it upside down, and gave it a knock on one of the family logs to dislodge a small rock. Then he put the boot back on and got up and started to walk towards Madam Tea-spill's beautiful caravan. It was the grandest caravan in the village. Handcrafted wooden flowers were inlaid into the wood around the door frame. Higher, above the layout of flowers, was the design of a heart-shaped cover the size of a man's heart, which pro-tected a secret wooden compartment. There was a keyhole in the centre of the cap. Only a special titanium key kept inside the Knight of Wishhearts locket could open it, thus causing the metal frame around this wooden heart to magically glow and turn, opening the secret cavity where the luminous almond-sized magical titanium lace heart lay. It was believed by the Gypsies that if a prince possessed this magical key a spell would come over him and lead him to the reigning Gypsy queen's caravan so he could unlock the wooden cavity, take out the titanium lace heart and give it to the Gypsy princess as a sign of love. Once wed they would replace the key and the lace heart into the spots embedded for them inside the Knight of Wishhearts locket, as a sign of union and love for each other. But if the titanium frame was destroyed or missing the cavity would remain locked forever.

Teaspill's caravan had a wooden sign that leaned on one of the large caravan wheels, it read: Madam Teaspill's Palm History Readings. Footmeyer always found this quite eerie.

The wood on Teaspill's caravan had a soft pearl-grey shine to it. Her aged horse was different shades of grey, he seemed a little odd. His strange metallic ears didn't seem real and he looked like he was made from metal. The old Gypsy queen sat below the open door of her caravan on the top step. She would play her squeeze box and sing an old Gypsy love song that brought back memories of her beloved dead husband, Tharpe, who was murdered many years ago, brutally beheaded by the sword of the Tainted Knight, Horrible Horribin.

The elusive woman had white hair that was braided around the crown of her head, thin strands lay upon her shoulders. Her eyes were shaped like a cat's and looked like a kaleidoscope of purple glass. Her skin was softly weathered. Etched upon her face were fine lines that reflected the story of her past. Painted wooden bracelets encircled her wrists and an old lace patchwork cotton dress, torn at the seams, covered her round plump body. She'd worn this dress every day since the love of her life, Tharpe, was killed. It was a special gift from him long, long ago. Wrapped around her head was a purple satin scarf to keep her warm. On her shoulders lay a dirty white woollen shawl filled with holes and pinned at the nape with a deformed purple crocheted flower given to her by her daughter Isa when she was a little girl. Teaspill could hardly walk now. Her legs were swollen and her slippers barely covered her big crooked feet. A wise and strange old woman.

"Good evening, Madam Teaspill," said Footmeyer, greeting her.

"Good evening, Charlie old boy. Saving the best for last?" she said jokingly.

"You are too wise," replied Footmeyer.

"Another wonderful celebration you have arranged as always, my dear friend," exclaimed Teaspill.

"Yes, and a particularly special one it will be this time around," Footmeyer said with a big smile on his face.

"Yes, I'm sure it will be," Madam Teaspill responded, then added, "Garth and Isa told me that they left an invitation to King Isaac and Queen Annette for tomorrow's celebration and proposed they betroth their new baby, if she is a girl, to their son Benjamin, the young Prince of Zymurgy."

"And they will agree?" questioned Footmeyer.

"Garth and Isa said King Isaac and his wife accepted the invitation. Let the rest be a mystical moment for Ecae," Teaspill chanted wisely.

"Yes! See you tomorrow, Madam," replied Footmeyer, turning away. "Oh, she haunts me sometimes," he said to himself as a shiver raised the hairs on the back of his neck.

The sun had almost set; Footmeyer walked over to Garth and Isa's caravan. Above the door was a sign that read, Garth and Isa Woods. Their caravan was made of light brown wood and the door had a beautiful stained glass window designed by Garth, with sweet peas inlaid into the glass. Footmeyer noticed a cinnamon strand tied to the door knob outside. He smiled, it was a sign that they had gone to the pond. Then he turned and headed back to the village centre. Isa would often bring back a bottle of water from the pond to wash her mother's hair. Teaspill told her the titanium flecked water was magical and gave all the Gypsy queens a strong and peaceful feeling.

Garth and Isa spent many long summer days as children playing inside the big tree trunk. On warm sunny days they would slide down a huge slate of rock and swim in the cool water of Slippery Slate Pond, but tonight, tonight was one of the most wonderful moments in Garth and Isa's life together, for Isa was heavy with child. Together, holding hands, they rested inside the cool darkness of the tree trunk. Garth asked Isa to close her eyes and hold out her hands. From his breast jacket pocket he pulled out a small leather bag and put it in her hands. She opened her eyes, reached inside the bag and took out a pair of soft little grey leather baby booties. He told Isa he'd made them himself. And that inscribed on the soles were the words, 'OUR ECAEP CHILD love Garth'.

"They're adorable, thank you," Isa said, gently laying them down on a big root. She put her arms around Garth and her head on his big strong shoulders. "I'm afraid, Garth," Isa whispered as she shivered.

"Don't be afraid," Garth consoled her, and kissed her hand. "You will be a wonderful mother and a splendid queen."

"Garth, tomorrow I will become queen, but my mother," Isa sighed, "she is growing so old. When she is gone her love is gone, and she will not see her grandchild grow up."

"Isa, love never goes away. Be calm," he said, and took her in his arms and held her closely. "Teaspill will be there tomorrow and eventually, like all of the other people of the village, she will travel up high into the night air with the warm purple flames of the Gypsy fires."

Isa felt comforted and nodded as Garth tightened the shawl around her slight shoulders. The young couple patiently waited for the big bonfire in the village to be lit before they rejoined the others in the village.

Meanwhile, the two villains were waiting impatiently for sundown. It was too late now but Horrible had contemplated getting his sword from his castle, a camouflaged junk domain held together with ancient pieces of joisting equipment. This strange looking structure hung from thick clanging chains and was lodged between two gigantic trees and supported on a horizontal outcropping of rock on the side of a mountain.

"If this plan fails it will be your fault!" Horrible said loudly. Shway's body stiffened. He thought that Horrible had gone crazy, knowing his sword was missing.

"Soon these insignificant little Gypsies will set their own lovely village on fire…" Horrible laughed, spitting wickedly through his rotten gritted teeth, "then we'll smash their walls into tiny little pieces." Shway went into shock and the colour drained from his face.

"Then you, Shway, will finish smashing the walls and meet me back here in this same spot, after I kill the old queen and steal the Gypsy heirloom locket necklace," Horrible added.

"What's an heirloom?" asked Shway naively.

"You stupid, stupid!…" Horrible yelled. He couldn't bear his partner's stupidity.

The two villains climbed upon their horses, fully clad in their suits of armour they waited and watched for the exact right time to begin their attack.

Only a faint red glow could be seen off to the west of the village. The sun had finally set. Garth and Isa were still inside the hollowed tree trunk holding hands, waiting for Footmeyer to light the big bonfire. Then they would go back and join the rest of the people in their village. At the same time, Footmeyer was waiting for Garth and Isa to return before lighting the fire, but the villagers wanted the fire to get started.

"Footmeyer, you're getting old!" someone yelled. "Let someone else light the fire!" They all laughed at this. All the families were gathered around the big firepit. Madam Teaspill sat on her special family log bench. Tapping one of her old feet, she began to lead the Gypsies into a famous old song while playing her squeeze box joyfully.

Footmeyer finally gave in, pulled a large match from the pocket of his overalls and struck it on his wooden leg, then held it to the kindling. It usually took a few minutes to start, but not tonight—the piled up logs caught on fire at once. Everyone cheered. They had never before seen Footmeyer make such a huge fire as this one. They sang loudly as the fire got bigger and bigger.

As Isa watched the bonfire glowing from the village centre, Garth slid his warm arms around her tummy. The fire looked so inviting, but for some unusual reason it started getting bigger and bigger. Horrible and Shway took off and were now smashing the wall.

"Look at it! My father is really outdoing himself tonight," remarked Garth.

"No...no, something is wrong," Isa said with deep concern.

The fire was beginning to spread along the ground, all around the caravans. The wheels of their homes snapped and sizzled, and the purpleberry bushes were burning like wildfire. Shrill screams came from the mouths of the children while fear froze upon their faces. Garth realized that something awful had happened.

"Isa, stay here near the waterfall!" he told her. "I'm going in to help!"

"No!" she screamed. "I'm coming with you!"

"No, you're not!" he commanded. "You'll be safe here, I'll come back for you!" He pulled her into his arms, kissed her, then raced out toward the centre of the village.

As Garth ran he could hear thunderous sounds coming from outside the walls as Horrible yelled and commanded Shway to smash them. Nothing gave Shway more pleasure than to strike the wall with his heavy flail until not one piece of it was left standing. A small section of the wall collapsed and fell into the pond.

People were running for their lives as the wind drove the fire through the trees like the hot breath of a fierce dragon.

When Garth reached the village centre he

helped the men who were using the horse's drinking buckets to throw water onto the fire. They quickly realized they had no chance of stopping the blaze. The people in the village ran through the hollow tree and down by the pond to escape. Desperate screams came from the women. The men were helping everyone get out of the village safely. Garth called out for his mother and father and went running around through the thick smoke desperately trying to find them.

Meanwhile, Madam Teaspill had suspected foul play. She'd stayed put on her family log bench and pulled her cue ball-sized crystal ball out of her pocket. She could see two crazed knights on horseback riding around the outside of the village, smashing the wall. Just as she suspected, it was the infamous Tainted Knight—Horrible Horribin. Wise old Teaspill knew he had come for the Gypsy heirloom locket necklace, the Knight of Wishhearts, and, as before, may try and claim another Gypsy's head. The crystal ball showed Horrible leaving his accomplice's side. He rode in toward the centre of the village, coming through the thick smoke that filled the grounds. He tied his horse to an old mossy tree.

Teaspill put the crystal ball back into her pocket. She realized a spell was in order to protect the precious necklace.

The Tainted Knight was no match for Teaspill. The cunning old Gypsy woman lay down and rested on the family log bench and waited for him to approach her.

Horrible strutted amongst the shadows and smoke looking for Teaspill. He searched around her strange ancient caravan. Finally he spotted the dark lumpy shape of a person who was lying down upon a log bench by the huge firepit.

Teaspill could hear the clanging sound of the Tainted Knight's metal suit. He was walking right up behind her. Horrible couldn't stand the heat from the fires burning around him. His body was sweltering hot inside his big heavy suit. He walked boldly around the log bench to see if it was Teaspill. He recognized her right away.

"You…queen of the Gypsies…get up!" Horrible demanded.

She didn't move. It was as though she

was dead. He poked her with the end of his cane, heeding the tales of the Gypsies. It was then that the despicable knight knelt down, removed his glove, and snatched the beautiful locket necklace off of Teaspill's neck. Then, standing up, he dropped it down inside the chest of his knight's suit.

Suddenly Teaspill sprang up, and with her bony old hands she clutched the forearms of Horrible's warm metal suit. Out of her mouth exuded a potent mist of titanium Gypsy breath which filled the Tainted Knight's helmet. He backed away, feeling disoriented. Teaspill had cast a spell which would cause the necklace to disappear within minutes of him riding off and would magically bring it back to safety upon her neck. Horrible turned away and hurried back to his horse, untied the big animal from the tree and victoriously rode off to find Shway.

Teaspill lay back down weakly on her family log bench.

Shway had long finished smashing the wall and had been hiding in the trees waiting for Horrible. He'd gotten sidetracked when he caught sight of Garth running around yelling and had been watching him to see what he was doing.

There was so much smoke throughout the village that Garth had given up searching for anyone. The Perfumavan had exploded and the only thing left of Miss Tressy's Hairavan was the burned out hulk of the caravan and four burning wheels. Golly Sweetman's caravan of sweets was burnt to a crisp. Even Tressy's smelly poultice lay smouldering on the ground—it was the worst thing Garth had ever smelled. He kicked it aside. Garth noticed Hans the clock had fallen over and was laying on his side with his centre burnt out. Garth turned around and went running back to get Isa when he tripped about twenty feet from Teaspill's caravan.

As Garth got up he noticed a shiny piece of metal on the ground. It was the heart-shaped titanium frame from Teaspill's caravan, it had fallen out somehow. He quickly scooped it up and put it in his pocket. Just as he did he heard the sound of galloping hoofbeats coming fast towards him and suddenly, out of nowhere, a giant set of long gangly arms grabbed him from behind and heaved him inside a partially burnt out caravan. With a loud thud someone bolted the caravan door shut. Laying on the floor Garth noticed he had been locked inside his own home.

"What is going on here?" he cried out.

Horrible came riding up to Shway, who was harnessing his horse to what was left of Garth and Isa's caravan. The two rogues had completed their despicable deed.

"I have great news," Horrible boasted. "I...have...the heirloom!" He reached down inside his knight suit, but the Gypsy heirloom locket necklace was an illusion that had magically disappeared. Horrible felt everywhere inside his suit. He glared at Shway with hatred in his eyes. He turned his horse around to go back to hunt for the necklace.

"I found it! We have it! I...uh...saw that Gypsy I caught, stuff it in his pocket," Shway called out proudly. Horrible's eyes darted about in their sockets in confusion.

"Good job, Shway!" Horrible said, shocked at his accomplice's deed and not able to understand how the necklace had fallen out of his metal suit. "Take what's left of this burning little hovel of wood and drag it back to my castle," Horrible commanded.

The smell of smouldering wood filled the inside of the dark caravan. Garth rubbed his eyes—they were irritated and stinging—but he couldn't see anything so he listened intently. He couldn't recognize the voices of the men on the outside who had captured him and locked him in his own home.

When Shway finished lashing on to the caravan, Horrible turned his horse to the road, gave out a wicked laugh of triumph and charged like a wild man out and over the rubble of the smashed village wall, galloping off into the night. Shway mounted his horse, nudged him forward, and started dragging Garth's caravan out of the village, following along behind his infamous master.

In the caravan Garth felt a warmth growing at his midsection. He looked down and saw an outline of the metal heart-shaped frame he had earlier put in his pocket. A strange warm glow was coming from it. Then, suddenly, it turned ice cold and a scratchy tingling sensation caught hold of his throat. Garth clutched at his Adam's apple.

There was a powerful tight constriction, not in his breathing which was full and wide open, but he couldn't utter a sound. Now a new fear swept through him. As a child he had heard the legend. If anyone other than the Gypsy queen removes or has possession of the heart-shaped frame that locks in the titanium lace heart, the ancient Gypsy ghost queen's curse of silence will possess them. They will be able to hear, but they cannot speak. And the only way to break the spell was to save a fellow Gypsy's life and return the frame to its place. Garth tried to clear his throat but no sound came out. With all-out energy he tried to yell. Nothing. He agonized about how terrible everything had become so quickly. He pulled the frame out of his pocket but it was too dark in the caravan to see it. It felt normal, just like an ordinary piece of metal. He had no intention of stealing the frame, he was actually trying to save it. Nothing made sense. Somehow he had to escape and find Isa. He put the heart-shaped frame back into his pocket. Then the caravan jolted to a halt and there was a loud clanging and banging from outside.

They had arrived at Horrible's castle. Shway unhitched his horse then manoeuvred the caravan onto a lift.

"Pull him up," Horrible ordered, as the caravan was lifted up on an unsteady, rusty metal lift. Finally the lift halted. Garth could hear the sound of metal doors opening up.

"Welcome home," Horrible called out sarcastically to Garth, in a gruff voice that echoed from within his helmet. "Shway, light the lanterns," Horrible demanded. "We have so much to learn about each other. Yes! Great knight captures crazy Gypsy man who sets his own village on fire." Horrible laughed hard.

"But, I thought we?..." Shway spoke up proudly.

"Be quiet, you fool!" snapped Horrible.

Garth slowly got up off his knees and looked out through a broken section of the window in the caravan door. He could see two fully clad knights in their suits of armour standing in front of it.

As Garth peered through the broken window he could only see the tips of hundreds of old rusted swords that were hanging from the ceiling by chains, pointing downwards to the floor. Out of Garth's view were parts of ancient weapons strangely formed to make weird metal clothes and furniture. Tables were filled with old pieces of armour. Shelves were filled with displays of child-like toy warriors, jousting on their horses with miniature ancient weapons.

Pieces of old armour hung from metal walls which had no windows. Garth couldn't see much through the broken caravan window. However, he could see in a far off corner a pedestal with the shiniest metal suit of armour he had ever laid eyes on, and a huge metal sword laying across the pedestal in front of the knight's boots. Garth slowly backed away from the window. Outside the caravan Horrible came closer to the window, stepped up on the caravan's partially burnt top step and, lifting up his chin piece, peered in at the young Gypsy man and spoke sarcastically in a low stern manner.

"Do you like my domain?"

Garth's throat was numb and when he tried to answer, nothing came out. He nodded his head up and down to gesture yes.

"No, you don't!" Horrible yelled. "Oh! Don't get shy on me now!" he mocked.

Garth slowly shook his head back and forth gesturing no and taking his index finger he pointed to the inside of his mouth.

"Shway, come here, look...look. What...is...he doing?" Horrible demanded.

Shway removed his big heavy helmet and dropped it to the floor. It made a huge clang throughout the room. Then, he strutted over toward Horrible with an attitude of, 'no problem, I'll take care of this boss'. With his heavy metal boots and armour still on, Shway awkwardly lifted one of his long legs and stepped onto the bottom burnt step. He bent over and looked in the cracked out piece of the window. Heads together, the two watched Garth trying to show them he couldn't speak. With the index finger of his right hand he pointed first to his right eye, then into his mouth, shaking his head side to side to gesture he couldn't speak. Finally, he pointed straight at Horrible. Shway started to make this into a game of charades and speculated on each one of Garth's actions.

"First word...eye. Second word...ate.

Third word, you. I…ate…you? No…wait!"
Shway yelled. "I've got it! I've got it!
I…hate…you! I knew it! He hates you!"
Then he laughed uncontrollably.

"Get…away…from the window!" Horrible yelled, shoving Shway off the step. "He can't speak, you ninny!" Then he mumbled to himself.

"The Gypsy's throat must be damaged from the fire. Drat! This will take forever to heal. Maybe…he's tricking me." Then he addressed Garth in an unsympathetic tone.

"Permanent confinement to your burnt little hovel should soon bring forth some conversation and, by the way, as artful as you may seem, I know that you picked up the Gypsy heirloom and shoved it in your pocket." Horrible then removed his heavy helmet and placed it on the burnt top step of the caravan. "Now, be a good little Gypsy and give it to daddy," he said impatiently, raking his metal glove across the singed wooden door.

As he held up his glove to the window he waited for Garth to hand it over. Garth slowly reached down into his pocket and pulled out the titanium heart frame, hoping that once he gave it up he might be set free so he could go back and save Isa.

Garth handed Horrible the precious frame that belonged to the secret compartment above Madam Teaspill's caravan door, it barely fit through the broken piece in the window. He knew he could never forgive himself for giving it to this evil man.

"Ah, ha! The moment I've been waiting for all my life," said Horrible. As he took the frame he closed his eyes and kissed it in victory, then opened his eyes to admire the one thing that was going to make him the most powerful man in all the land. "What is this?" yelled Horrible, horrified. Shway hurried forward and took a closer look at the metal object in the hands of his master.

"Oh! Oh," Shway grumbled. "It's a metal cookie cutter," he speculated, shrugging his shoulders and pulling cowardly away, his eyes squinting sideways at Horrible.

Horrible threw it at Shway, missing him. The object fell to the floor. Shway retrieved it as it clanged and rolled along the floor.

"But you love metal," said Shway tenderly.

"Put it down," demanded Horrible as his eyes protruded from his skull.

Shway very gently placed the metal heart frame on a nearby table. Horrible was livid. He moved over as close to the caravan window as his large nose could get.

"Where is the locket?" Horrible demanded of Garth.

Garth pulled his empty pockets inside out, but still couldn't speak a word.

"It's ok sir, we can try again tomorrow," Shway said, trying not to imagine what was coming next.

Horrible then exploded with an angry yell so loud it echoed multiple times off the walls. He threw his ancient Morning Star flail high up into the hanging swords. They clanged in a domino effect. Powdered red chunks of rust rained downward upon the floor.

Garth thought back to when he was a young boy. He remembered his father, Footmeyer, telling him the real story of how his leg went missing. Suddenly it all made sense. Garth knew he was a prisoner in the castle of the Tainted Knight, Horrible Horribin— the wickedest knight in all the lands—and at his mercy. As the clanging swords came to a stop, the room took on a deadly silence.

"You tricked me," growled Horrible. "If you don't tell me where the heirloom is I will chain you for all to see inside the tower in the town I own, the town of Metalville. You will remain my prisoner forever." Horrible laughed, an evil laugh, loud and hard.

Shway twirled what he thought was a metal cookie cutter with his pointer finger, looked at it, then walked over to the caravan, popped it back inside the hole in the window and retrieved his helmet, grinning at Garth pathetically.

"What are you doing?" snapped Horrible, swinging his cane at Shway.

Shway jumped sideways. "Missed me, missed me, now you have to kiss the cookie cutter," Shway sang under his breath sarcastically.

"Go put the horses away," said Horrible in a gruff defeated manner, then swaggered away. The two villains retired for the evening. As Shway snored the foul air stagnated in the room. One by one the lanterns burned themselves out. Garth could not sleep, all he could think about was if only he could get out and save Isa. Where would she go? Who would help her have their baby? A prisoner in his own caravan, Garth curled up in the corner. Sadness overcame his heart as he was locked away forever. The metal heart frame lay in front of Garth on the floor. He quietly picked it up and put it back in his pocket, the only memory of his home in the Gypsy village.

Earlier, back in the village, Isa was still waiting inside the tree trunk for Garth to return. She watched the smoke funnel high up into the cold night air. She didn't usually go against her husband's wishes but this time she was frightened and decided to go back in, to the fire in the village. The baby boots tumbled out of the tree stump and lay under a shrub; fear-ridden, Isa forgot them. Holding up her long dress so it wouldn't catch fire, she took large strides towards the village and the unbearable heat and smoke, covering her mouth and nose with the arm of her sleeve. As Isa reached the centre of the village she noticed her caravan was gone. Looking around fearfully, she called loudly for Garth. She could feel a heavy frosted dew starting to fall around her. A magical mist of frozen purple metallic droplets began to fall upon the whole village and diminish some of the fires. Isa looked towards the firepit and noticed a dark figure laying down on one of the family log benches. As she got closer she noticed it was Teaspill, her mother, and she became afraid. She cradled the sides of her stomach gently with her hands as sharp pains came from deep inside her womb.

"Tea, Tea, are you all right?" Isa said, out of breath as she ran towards her mother.

"Where is Garth?" she asked anxiously. Teaspill didn't move. She slowly opened her sore red eyes and squinted at Isa. "Mother, I can't find Garth," Isa repeated desperately.

"Garth is gone. They took him," Teaspill said weakly.

"Who, mother? Who took him?" Isa pleaded.

"The Tainted Knight," replied Teaspill as she closed her eyes, then opened them once again to focus on Isa's frightened face.

"The Tainted Knight! What will we do?" Isa exclaimed, as she gently held her hand to her mouth trying to catch her breath.

"Leave Isa, take my horse and caravan. Take the food box from underneath my caravan steps," Teaspill said in a weakened state.

"I cannot leave you here mother, you'll die. Let me help you up. Come with me, please," Isa begged her. "I won't leave without you."

Isa put her arms around the old woman to help her up.

"Please, get up," Isa said as she looked at her mother sadly.

"I am old, Isa, too old to travel far. The warm purple flames of the Gypsy fires are calling my name," chanted Teaspill. "Isa, take my purple scarf, wear it as a sign of Ecae." Isa graciously took the scarf and put it gently to her cheek, the warm sweet scent of her mother's perfume on it calmed her heart. Isa then pulled her cloak hood over her chilled head and tied the scarf around her neck in a bow. "Go north to the high hills, to the castle of Zymurgy and get help," Teaspill continued. She was failing quickly and could feel the dense beat of her heart, fading like the distant sound of a drum.

Isa looked at her mother with tears in her eyes. She knelt down beside her, held her hand and kissed her lovingly on the fore-head, then laid her head softly upon the old woman's shoulder and gave her one last hug. Standing up slowly she raised her head and looked over towards her mother's horse and caravan.

"Goodbye, mother," Isa said sadly. "I love you, we loved each other." Tears came from Isa's beautiful eyes and rolled down her cheeks into the corners of her mouth.

After saying her final goodbye, Isa did as her mother told her to. She curtsied to her mother, the old queen of the Gypsies, then turned and walked over to Teaspill's strange old cob horse. She wondered why he was still waiting by the caravan as though he had been summoned to attend to her needs. The caravan had suffered little damage; one front wheel had been partially burnt but could still be used to travel a short distance.

Isa climbed up and put the food box on the caravan's bench, noticing that a partially scorched tree branch had fallen onto the front of the caravan just above the door where the wooden heart was. A small piece of wood had been chipped off but she didn't realize that the heart-shaped metal frame was gone. She shivered from the cold wind as she struggled to lift the branch and let it fall to the side. How lucky, she thought, that the caravan itself had not burnt to the ground as so many others had. She watched her warm breath rise as a mist into the cold night air, shivered again as the wind made a haunting and mournful cry as it swept around the caravan. It was dark and getting colder, she felt a strong movement within her womb. There is no time to waste, she told herself. With fear and near panic, Isa hitched Teaspill's horse to the caravan then climbed back up to the seat, took the reins, gave them a gentle flick, and the horse started pulling the caravan. It was getting really cold now. Isa tightened Teaspill's purple scarf to keep her warm. Leaving the village she steered the horse and caravan over the smashed rubble of the wall that lay scattered upon the ground. Holding her head high she tried to be brave but the sadness was too much, her tears fell as she looked over her shoulder. The thought of leaving her mother made her heart painfully heavy, she gave a meek wave to say goodbye to the village and her life there.

As soon as Teaspill was sure that Isa had gone on her way, the old Gypsy woman pushed herself up with all her might and sat up on the log bench. She had heard the gruff voices of the men yelling as they left the village. Horrible would now pay. The ancient Gypsy trick had worked and the Knight of Wishhearts heirloom locket was still upon Teaspill's neck. The day had finally come, one that she thought she'd never see, and the great Gypsy spell was now the only defence the weak old woman had. She managed to stand, looking high up to the sky, and took the precious locket—the Knight of Wishhearts—from her old wrinkled neck and held it into the night. Queen Teaspill knew the purple Gypsy flames awaited her. She'd lived an intriguing life, often searching her soul to help the ones she loved. Mirrored reflections of the past toiled within her mind as her white hair turned into brittle titanium strands. Her skin shrivelled and transformed to the colour of a black pearl, her dress and shawl turned into dark silver metallic titanium and with intensifying heat they produced cracks that glowed, then her body revolved slowly. Her weary eyes became spellbound and transformed into purple and grey kaleidoscopes, fixating on the stained glass Knight of Wishhearts locket necklace, magically reflecting it's many tranquil colours throughout the village, stopping the fires. Then she stopped turning. In front of her, high over the firepit, was a hovering vision of herself as a child, holding hands with other Gypsy children, gleefully dancing around a garden of sweet peas and singing Gypsy songs. A second vision appeared, a newborn baby crying from hunger, titanium tears beaded in the corners of her eyes. Finally, a grotesque vision appeared, one of terror. She clutched the Knight of Wishhearts locket necklace and held it to her bosom, by her heart, as the wicked Tainted Knight appeared right before her, holding his big metal sword high into the night with the bloody head of her murdered husband Tharpe on the end of it. Her head dropped in anguish. Now revengeful anger engulfed her. Raising her head high, the old Gypsy queen closed her eyes and spoke.

"With the strength of all the Titanium Gypsy Queens, a spell I cast upon this village and over the land of Zymurgy. On the first snow fall will come a noble king to save the Gypsy heirloom locket from the clutches of evil. I decree the next Gypsy princess be born with a transparent heart and on her sixteenth birthday a gift she shall receive, the stained glass Knight of Wishhearts locket, which will magically draw her back to the forest of Ecae. There her transparent heart will be enriched with beautiful colours when enchanted by her betrothed prince, who, with a special titanium key, will unlock the magical compartment causing the metal heart frame to turn, exposing the magical titanium lace heart. This he will give to her as a sign of love, it will set her heart aglow and in love she will be. If anything fails she will die and the Village of Ecae will remain gone forever."

Then, with a crackling sound, remnants of the caravan's ashes were absorbed far beneath the earth and any Gypsies left hiding in the forest were transmuted by a ribbon of purple mystical haze which sent them to live in freedom, up in the underside of the ancient tree stump to survive another existence.

As the spell spread throughout the land, ancient mummified Gypsy remains called Mipsies stirred inside the darkness of Silver Mountain and were vexed because the spell stopped the magical titanium spring water from flowing into the waterfall. And only by the grace of Teaspill did the Mipsie ghosts remain swaddled in their strange cocoons for, if the spell had warranted, the ancient ghosts of the Gypsy king and queen, along with the Mipsies, would have been released to wreak havoc over the land of Zymurgy.

Teaspill, now swaying back and forth, chanted as bright purple lightening struck the ground and loud thunderous booms stormed over the forest. The old woman chanted a spell, magnified in its ancient Gypsy form.

Oh, Gypsy wind, cast the kaleidoscope spell.
He ta le, she sa tee,
la lee, bring wind and rain.
Put out village fires,
let a new storm begin.
By the powers of Teaspill,
hide this village within.
He ba le, she sa tee,

ba le, bring snow with fire.
She sa tee, she sa tee,
purple Gypsy flames be gone! This night,
my daughter will transform to another life.
Into frozen sweet peas that grow upon the
ground,
where the Gypsy baby with the transparent
heart will be found.
For only true love and the key her prince brings,
will open the heart and let the colours pour in.
Then the Knight of Wishhearts will reign once
again.

As the purple metallic mist began to retreat into the night, Teaspill weakly collapsed upon the log bench. A huge bolt of white lightening struck her body and turned it into a magnificent pile of warm glowing silver titanium ashes and the heirloom locket necklace lay hidden beneath them. Some of the ashes began to trickle gently down off the now burnt log bench onto the ground. They swirled around into a circle. The wind brought them up into the air, then a small white cat suddenly appeared from the residue of the ashes. The little cat looked about the forested area with her big kaleidoscope eyes.

"Well, this is just not what I was expecting," said the cat in a spoiled manner. "Why, I'm not even a nice colour, I'm a scrawny dirty white cat." She was disgusted with her appearance. She reached up towards her nose with one of her paws and felt her whiskers. "My whiskers are metallic and stiff," she complained, as she crossed her eyes and looked down her nose to see the brittle glowing sticks. "A Persian cat in a forest, a faux paw," said the dirty little white cat. "Well, at least I have a fur coat." Off she scurried into the trees and disappeared into the frosty air as it began to snow, and snow, and snow.

FOUR

The Secret

Isa had now travelled a long way from the village, she was heading higher and higher into the hills. Looking back she could see a strange coloured lightening storm hovering over the village and wondered if it would be moving towards her. She wanted to turn back but knew she had to continue her journey to the castle of Zymurgy just beyond the hills. She was nearly halfway there.

Isa's beautiful black hair held a blue metallic tinge under the moonlight. She breathed in the cold night air and shivered. Her labour pains were getting stronger and stronger. Isa could only hope to reach the castle before her baby was born.

What once seemed so peaceful up in the highlands now became cold dead silence except for the sound of the horse hooves upon the rocky road and the crackling of the cold wooden caravan wheels on the hard frozen ground.

Isa's eyes followed her warm breath up into the night until it disappeared into the cold air. A faint union of stars haunted the sky. As Isa looked up at the moon she noticed the purple silhouette of a Gypsy queen inside the big bright ball.

"Oh, nonsense," Isa said, but, as a young girl she had heard the elders of the village tell the legendary story—when the Gypsy queen sleeps on the full moon a spell will be cast upon the land. "You're a beautiful moon," said Isa. "I think you are just made of cheese and cheese can't cast spells." She smiled at her thought.

Isa opened up her food box and took out a small piece of bread.

"I am so hungry," she said, and looked up at the moon. "If you're made of cheese and I have some bread, we will have a wonderful midnight picnic together."

Without another thought Isa ate the whole piece of bread. The big bright moon seemed to look down upon the brave young

Gypsy girl and began to sing her a song in a soft low voice.

Just a Gypsy girl, or are you a queen,
so gentle at heart a lovely manner it seems.
For time moves so slowly on this dark cold night,
I will guide you along with my soft moonlight.
Your rickety travelling dark little house,
is barely big enough for even a mouse.
A place awaits you beyond your dreams,
it will help you save her, my Gypsy queen.
Just a Gypsy girl or are you a queen,
so gentle at heart a lovely manner it seems.
For time moves so slowly on this dark cold night,
I will guide you along with my soft moonlight.
He will soon meet you so take on your plight,
He'll magically find you in the deep of the night.
In marriage a prince once took your hand,
now your new Gypsy babe will be queen of the land.
Just a Gypsy girl or are you a queen,
so gentle at heart a lovely manner it seems.
For time moves so slowly on this dark cold night,
I will guide you along with my soft moonlight.

The full moon shone down on the old cob horse pulling the caravan slowly up a rugged trail into the high hills with a lone girl huddled on the high seat holding the reins. Once again Isa looked up at the moon with soft grey eyes that were now getting sleepy. She was very tired. She thanked the moon for lending his company to her and noticed big dark shadows of grey clouds moving in to cover him. Tiny snowflakes began to fall.

"Oh, my, I am so cold!" She shivered, pulling the purple scarf closer to her delicate body.

The tired old horse struggled against a steepening incline on the constantly winding rocky trail through the highlands. Isa was startled that only a few feet higher in elevation the snow was coming down in a deluge. What had been a bright moon was now dimmed severely. She had to squint hard to see the trail and could make out only a few feet ahead. Everything else was deep dark black. And colder. The horse was straining with great difficulty, trying to pull the caravan up the steep hillside. Isa was pained with sympathy and kept up a kind constant chatter of encouragement to him. Finally they seemed to have reached a peak for the trail began to slope downward, it became easier going. Hard-packed snow and ice was underfoot. The horse slipped, veered hard to his right to keep from falling, then suddenly his traces broke free. Without control of any kind now the caravan picked up speed at once and freely rolled down the slope. In only a few seconds it jammed its front left wheel into a jagged boulder on the side of the trail with a loud cracking and splintering of wood. The wheel snapped off. The caravan teetered for an instant, then started to roll over. Isa was thrown to the ground and before she could pull herself out of the way the heavy caravan came crashing down, pinning her left leg under one of its back wheels. She was in extreme pain and couldn't pull her trapped leg free. Isa's stomach was very sore from the fall and she lay tightly bound under the wheel of the caravan. Riddled in pain she yelled for someone to help, but all that came to her was a faint echo of her own voice ringing out into the cold night. Her beautiful young eyes filled with tears as she held her stomach, then laid down and pushed her beautiful secret into the cold lonely night, giving birth to a Gypsy princess whose small cry filled the air. Covered in blood, Isa looked down at her newborn child then tried to sit up but was too weak.

"What way is this for you to arrive," Isa whimpered to the warm wiggly crying infant.

As painful as it was, Isa quickly removed her cloak and pulled it around the infant, then used her mother's purple scarf to make a bow around the bundled cloak to secure the warmth of the baby. Isa was trembling from shock, she was very weak. As she looked at her new baby she kissed her gently on her little nose. The baby was very pale and seemed to have no colour.

"You are beautiful, did you know? You are the new Gypsy princess. Yes, you are, and I am your m—" Isa stopped, holding her baby close against her breast, her body sinking into a state of frozen shock. Her eyes slowly closed. Isa cradled her new babe, then was embraced by death's arms.

Isa was too young to make the journey up into the purple flames of the Gypsy fires, and so a spell had come to pass from a wish she made as a child, that if she were to die young, could the great Gypsy queen's ghost find it in her heart to turn what was left of her into some pretty sweet peas, to grow all year round forever and ever. Magically, her body turned into a circle of beautiful frozen sweet peas. Bundled in Isa's cloak and secured by Teaspill's purple scarf, the baby lay in the centre of the flowers. The icy wind whipped at the caravan as the heavy snow continued and, in no time at all, completely covered the newborn in a soft mound of pure white.

Meanwhile, King Isaac had been travelling and was now returning on horseback to his home lands. Since the death of his mother and father he had become a brave, distinguished young king, still very tall and slight. His features were older now, but his hair still wild. His eyes, deep green with long auburn lashes, had wooed the heart of Miss Annette Gray into marriage. He held the wisdom of an old man. His clothing was that of an ancient marksman.

From a distance he noticed the dense purple

storm clouds over the Gypsy village. As Isaac approached the village he saw the walls had been destroyed, only a few pieces visible. He rode his horse towards the centre of the village. The ground was now getting covered with snow, but black soot lay under it. The smell of smoke still rose up from underneath the cold ground.

"Anyone here?" yelled Isaac. There was nothing but stone cold silence. Isaac saw something strange on a burnt log bench. He rode his horse closer to see what it was. He got off his horse and there upon the log bench was a mound of glowing metallic ashes. What was it, he thought to himself, it looked like strange glowing pieces of metal or rock.

He removed his riding gloves and put one of his hands over the ashes to see if they were hot. Warm, he thought to himself. Then he scooped some up into the palm of his hand to take a closer look. Some had fallen to the ground. In the centre of the metallic ashes lay the beautiful stained glass Knight of Wish-hearts locket. Isaac had seen this before, worn only by the Gypsy queens and, lastly, on the neck of Madam Teaspill. The locket must have accidentally fallen off, he thought. He'd listened but wasn't sure about all the Gypsy stories, but he knew enough not to leave the locket in the ashes. He picked it up, looked at it for a moment, then carefully put it into his inner coat pocket. He was perplexed, everything in the village was gone except this one burnt log bench.

"What horrible thing could have happened to these lovely people?" he said. Isaac got back up on his horse. He looked around and noticed there was not one caravan left in the whole village. Had they all been burnt down, he wondered. He rode out of the village, raced through the night, and headed up into the highlands into the snow. The brave king travelled swiftly, homeward bound. He veered off the road up a snowy hillside and took a shortcut through the forest.

Deeper into the woods he came upon an old horse standing asleep under a tree. It was branded with an 'E' and it looked like Madam Teaspill's horse. King Isaac approached the animal cautiously. When he got closer he saw that hanging from the horse's neck was a chain and on it was a medallion the size of a child's hand, upon which were etched the letters, KERMACK. The horse turned its head to look at him, as if he was trying to tell him something. Isaac cocked his head with renewed interest. The animal's shiny grey coat was eerie, it seemed to be emitting a dim light of its own.

"Come on, boy," Isaac coached him. Instead, the old horse turned away, took a few steps toward the road then stopped, as if to show the way to where Isa's caravan had tumbled down the steep slope.

"You're not as dumb as you look," Isaac commented, then steered his horse to the edge of the road and looked down. It was still snowing and difficult to see but he was certain that at the bottom of the ravine was an overturned Gypsy caravan.

"Anyone down there?" he yelled. There was no response. He yelled again, "Is anyone down there?" All he heard was his own muffled echo bouncing softly off the snow covered mountain. Isaac dismounted, led his horse to Kermack, and tied the two horses together. He then slid down the slope to the bottom of the gully where he found Teaspill's caravan overturned on its side. It was still snowing and difficult to see, but Isaac could make out that the caravan's door had been flung open and that the left front wheel had been smashed. He carefully climbed up to the seat and looked inside. All was darkness.

"Anyone in here?" he called out. He thought he heard the faintest cry and peered in closer, finding two round spots of glossy light in the cold darkness, two big round purple marble cat eyes. There sat what had become of Teaspill, a dirty little white cat with metallic whiskers who stared at Isaac with strange eyes. He reached in and gently picked up the cold odd-looking little creature, put it in his breast coat pocket and wondered how it had survived the cold. He climbed down, looked around at the wreckage in dismay, then started to make his way back up to the road. He had gotten about halfway up when he heard another muffled cry coming from below. He quickly scrambled down the embankment and started to climb back up onto the caravan when the cry came again. Isaac frowned, he thought it might be coming from under the caravan. He jumped down, got on his hands and knees and started brushing away the snow trying to feel his way under the wagon when, from below his gloved hands, came a dim iridescent glow. His hands swept across something brittle. Flowers. Beautiful solidly-frozen sweet peas appeared from beneath the snow.

"Flowers? In the middle of winter?" he asked himself. "How strange."

He heard the faint cry again, it seemed to be at his side. He turned and brushed away the snow from a small mound, uncovering a dark bundle, a cloak secured by a purple scarf tied into a bow. Another cry came from the bundle. He picked it up. King Isaac's heart was pounding as he untied the bow and pulled apart the frozen material. He was astonished to find a new born baby girl still smeared with birth blood. Where's your mother, he wondered. He knew Isa was heavy with child. This must be the new Gypsy princess, Isaac guessed. The baby's cry was weak. Isaac quickly wrapped her back up in the cloak, tied the purple scarf around it and slipped the frozen bundle inside his warm hunting jacket. He carefully got to his feet. "Your mother has to be somewhere," he said to himself, looking all around, finding no one. He felt his way all around the wrecked Gypsy caravan, calling out, "Is anyone here? Hello? . . ." He listened. Only the cold wind and snow beat against his face.

In sadness King Isaac climbed back up the slope to the road, crossed to the two horses tied together, carefully mounted his horse, then made sure that the dirty little white cat and nearly frozen newborn babe tucked inside his coat were warm and secure. He turned his horse to the road, with Madam Teaspill's old horse, Kermack, trailing behind on a lead, and made his way down from the highlands towards home.

On the way down through the hills the snow eased up and King Isaac pondered on the problem of what to do with the infant he could feel wriggling once in a while against his bosom. It was only as he was halfway back that a brilliant and kind idea popped into his head. He turned his powerful horse around, held Kermack tight, and followed a switchback that took him a half hour south of the Gypsy village to where the middle-aged spinster twins, Rosey and Posey, lived on a small farm and operated a nursery specializing in a large variety of flowers for all seasons. Isaac held a great fondness for the two sisters, having known them since he was a little boy when they would deliver beautiful flowers to the castle for all occasions. No one would know better about how to deal with the situation than Rosey and Posey, even better than Queen Annette or the busy staff at the castle. Isaac steered the horses through the cold night over snowbound hills that led him towards the humble abode known as Flower Petal Cottage.

FIVE

Flower Petal Cottage

Prepared for what was the worst winter ever, Flower Petal Cottage withstood the dreadful snow fall. This was the home of the spinster twins, Rosey and Posey. Inside this sturdy cottage was a large cast iron wood-burning stove that kept the two women nice and cosy. They sat in their rocking chairs on each side of the stove, having their evening tea. Dressed in their cotton nightshirts and satin nightcaps, they watched the lanterns flicker as the wind whistled in through the tiny cracks of the cottage walls.

Rosey was tall and skinny, an unattractive middle-aged woman with fire red hair and small beady brown eyes. As she sat in her rocking chair, her long skinny body looked like a stripe down the centre of it. Her bony ankles cracked as she moved her big feet back and forth inside her favourite red knitted slippers. Rosey had a cranky disposition and was very bossy, always ordering Posey about.

Posey was the most attractive of the twins. Her short curly brown hair hugged her sweet round chubby face. She was cute and plump but she lacked intelligence. Her fat little fingers and broad little feet moved nervously as she rocked carefully, sipping her hot tea and nibbling on sweet cakes. She watched her sister knit another misshapen project, like the slippers which Rosey had made for her. They were too big and kept sliding off her feet. Posey called her sister Rosebud. She thought the nickname might sweeten up her sour disposition. Posey was a very jolly gal and loved to giggle.

Rosey was often cranky and used to think to herself that if Posey wasn't her sister, she might have taken her out and abandoned her in the forest a long time ago.

Posey often doused herself with freesia-scented talcum powder, which she made herself from the flowers in the garden. Sometimes her dark side would come out and she would load up with lots of talcum powder, knowing that Rosey was allergic to it. With not very much in common, except for the fact the two were family, they managed to run the best nursery in the land.

It was getting late now. Rosey rolled up the shawl she was knitting and put it in a box beside her rocking chair, a tired yawn came out of her large mouth.

"I'm going to bed now," she said.

"Me too," agreed Posey, yawning.

"You know how you need your beauty sleep," Rosey said sarcastically.

"But first, I'm going to finish my tea," giggled Posey, and she tipped her teacup upon her lower lip, sipped the last drop from the bottom of it and stretched out her plump short legs. She tried to get up out of her rocking chair but her bottom got stuck in between the two arms of it. She wiggled her way out, nearly falling on the floor.

"Oh, my, too many sweet breads," she said to herself.

She shuffled over to the sink in her cosy slippers, left her cup, then took the last lit lantern and went upstairs to bed. Every night before the two women would retire, Rosey would head up the creaky stairwell first, with a lit lantern to find her way, and yell out in a bossy voice.

"Is the big wooden door locked, and have you blown out all the lanterns?"

"Yes, Rosebud," Posey would reply obediently, and off to bed she would go.

It was an unusually cold snowy night. Posey snuffed out the lantern on her night table. She put one of her short legs on her bed step and sprung herself into bed, then pulled the covers right up around her neck and watched the big snowflakes blow by the frozen window pane. She was glad she had remembered to put an extra woollen blanket on her bed. Everything was peaceful inside Flower Petal Cottage.

"Goodnight Rosebud," called Posey sweetly.

"Goodnight Posey," answered Rosey glibly.

No sooner had they wished each other a goodnight than a knock came from outside the cottage's front door. Posey got out of bed and hurried over to the window to look outside, but only saw a glistening blanket of snow covering the ground.

"I think I hear something outside," she

whispered, watching the snow fall. "Why, I'm sure I hear the meowing of a kitten, poor little thing out there in the snowstorm. Rosey!" she called out, "I hear a kitten crying outside."

"It's only the wind," replied Rosey, "remember, you need your beauty rest. Go back to sleep."

The haunting cry of a kitten filled Posey's head with awful thoughts.

"Listen, can you hear it?" she called to her sister again.

"I think you ate too many sweets," Rosey said critically and, getting annoyed at the nonsense, she pulled her nightcap down over her ears and closed her eyes tightly.

"All right," said Posey, disappointed, for she loved kittens. Back into bed she climbed once again and under the covers.

The cry came again but this time it was louder. Posey sat up quickly and listened. She was going to get to the bottom of this herself.

"Rosey isn't always right," she mumbled to herself, and quietly pulled back her covers. She slid down onto the cold wooden floorboards and, barefoot, not making a sound, she tiptoed over to the squeaky old bedroom door. Posey shivered from nerves. She gently opened the door with her small chubby hands. The cry came again.

"I knew it!" said Posey, quickly covering her mouth with her hand. She tiptoed towards her snoring sister's bedroom, quietly closed the door, then headed straight back along the hallway and down the creaky staircase into the kitchen. She lit a lantern on a table to give her some light. The cry was coming from outside the big wooden front door.

"Poor little thing," Posey said in a whisper.

Posey remembered what Rosey had told her about opening the door to strangers.

"Oh, a mere little kitten couldn't hurt anyone," she thought, and slowly unbolted the big wooden door. The wind blew it wide open and snow came blowing in through the doorway. Posey wasn't sure if she was shaking from the cold or afraid of what Rosey would do when she found out she had opened the door. She saw something on the porch in front of her.

"I knew it!" Posey said again, ecstatically.

There on the doorstep was a bundled package with a frozen purple scarf tied around it. Beside it sat a freezing scruffy white cat with strange eyes that were staring Posey right in the face.

"Oh, come here," said Posey.

As she bent over to pick up the cat it hissed at her then ran off into the snowstorm. Posey watched the cat disappear with a swirl into the dark frozen night.

"Oh, darn," Posey scowled.

As Posey bent down to pick up the package she heard a muffled cry. It startled her. Posey carried the bundle inside and put it on the floor.

"Can I help?" asked Rosey as she rocked slowly in her chair, glaring at her sister.

"Ahh!" Posey screamed. "No, ah, yes, please," said Posey tensely.

"You scared me!" she added.

"Really," answered Rosey sarcastically, as she went over and bolted the door shut. "And...I hope no one opens it again tonight." Looking at Posey, she rolled her eyes.

"Why didn't you help me?" asked Posey angrily.

"I was busy watching you making a spectacle out of yourself. Now, why would I interfere when you're being scared half to death? That wouldn't be nice, would it?" said Rosey in a snippety manner.

"No, it wouldn't," replied Posey, turning her nose up in the air. "Let's open it, it looks like a present. I bet it's kittens."

Rosey glared at her. The two women knelt down on the floor in the dim light of the kitchen and Posey untied the purple scarf that bound the bundle. A faint muffled cry came from within and the bundle wriggled just a little. Posey held her breath with excitement. She gently pulled open the black wool cloak and there was a newborn baby with dried birth blood on her shrivelled skin, her thin little body was as white as a ghost. A purple sweet pea flower lay next to her tiny ear. Rosey and Posey looked at each other as if they had seen a ghost.

At the same time they said, "A baby?"

Posey got the hot water and Rosey folded the tea towels into diapers. After the shock had worn off their motherly instincts kicked in and they decided to give the baby a nice warm bath.

"She looks rather pale, doesn't she?" asked Posey. "Maybe she was born in the forest, maybe she's a blessing in disguise."

"Maybe not," Rosey shrugged unhelpfully. "Well!…we'll never know where she came from…will we? Or who left her on our doorstep!"

The baby was unusually beautiful but, as they bathed her, they noticed her hair was filled with a fine grey film of dust, and no matter how many times they washed it, it wouldn't come clean.

"Her hair is odd," said Rosey.

"It's only baby hair," replied Posey.

After many attempts to clean her dusty hair the two sisters decided to cover her head with a delicate woollen sock and wrap her in a small bright red woollen blanket to keep her warm for the night.

Rosey put a couple more logs in the stove and headed for the stairs, leaving her sister with the newborn baby.

"Goodnight Posey," said Rosey.

Sweet, tender-hearted Posey cradled the tiny baby in her arms, rocking her chubby body back and forth gently, lovingly. The infant twisted and cried out. "Oh my, the poor little thing must be hungry," she muttered. Holding the baby in one arm she managed to pour some sweet milk from the cooler into a small saucepan, then put it on the stove to warm.

"Ohh!...Now, don't you fret," said Posey, pacing back and forth about the sitting room, bouncing the baby on her bosom and patting its little back as it cried from hunger. "Mommy is—" Realizing what she had inferred, Posey stopped a quick second, and furrowed her brow. "Mother?...Oh, dear!...A mother...Never mind!" she said, patting the baby even quicker, with tears welling up in her eyes. "Auntie Posey...a...and...Auntie Rosey...will take care of everything." Holding the infant in her left arm, she scooped a spoon into the milk and tested it. "Mmmm...just right, nice and warm!" she chortled, then sat down with the baby in her rocking chair which was in easy reach of the stove. "Now, let's see if this works," Posey proposed. She reached over to the stove and dipped the small finger of her right hand into the pan of milk, then pulled it out and pressed it gently at the baby's mouth. The infant got the idea quickly and hungrily began to suckle small droplets of warm milk from Posey's little finger. Again and again this was repeated until finally the babe's hunger was gone. Posey rocked back and forth gently in the chair looking down at the sleepy infant, a flood of instincts welling up within her. She had never before experienced a feeling so deeply satisfying. In her tone-deaf voice she began to sing to the infant and soon managed to put the baby and herself to sleep on that cold winter night.

❧✕❧

SIX

The Garden Shed

The morning dew glistened on the faces of the many beautiful flowers that were blooming in the garden around Flower Petal Cottage.

Posey scurried about, decorating an old kitchen table with a pretty crossed-stitched cotton country tablecloth. Laid upon it was a freshly polished silver tea service, three fine linen serviettes, butter knives, and three pretty porcelain flower-printed tea cups.

As Valena awakened in her bed she slowly opened her big soft grey eyes. She studied the dust particles that floated amidst the golden rays of sunlight that shone in through her small partially-open bedroom window. All of a sudden she heard something fumbling and fluttering about outside, then it plopped itself inside the opening of the window and, with a thump, landed on a ledge behind the lace curtains. Valena looked to see what it was and she spied two sets of kooky looking bugs, eyes peeking in through the worn curtain to see if she was awake. Pushing back her patchwork quilt she hurried over to the window and, quickly pulling back the curtain, she startled the two peculiar small bugs known as Quimmy Boinks. These small creatures were Valena's secret friends, who she'd never told anyone about. They lived out in the forest a ways from Flower Petal Cottage. These two unusual hairy bugs had large furry grey pussy willow wings on their backs and were the height of a wooden baking spoon, with limbs the thickness of the spoon's round stick handle. Except, they were shiny and silver in colour. These two Quimmies' names were Tic and Toc. They were brothers, and were a little cuckoo because they were crazy about time, most of the time. But right now they seemed to be having a hard time giving a very important invitation to Valena.

"Your Highness, excuse our timeliness," they said together, bowing to Valena.

"Good morning!" chirped Valena. "You're a long way from home."

"It's time…for a party," said Toc. "It's time…to celebrate. It's—," Tic covered Toc's mouth with his candy-like, brightly glowing coloured hand. "Go, stop. Go…Stop," continued Toc, dodging Tic's hand.

"We have no time for talking! Just show the TIME!" said Tic.

Valena laughed at them. They were cute but unbelievably crazy!

"OK…I'll time us. We'll start in five seconds…GO!" said Toc.

Toc pointed straight up in the air with one of his short arms. Tic was moving one of his long arms in a big circle in front of his body, trying to imitate a clock hand and show the right time that Valena's party was going to start, but it was way too crazy and confusing for Valena to understand. They moved their arms in many different positions, even counter-clockwise indicating the clock's time was haywire and on full speed, then they sang hurriedly to her.

A party in the forest, as strange as it may seem,
where magical things can happen, like gifts and
secret things.
No time, no time, no reason or rhyme,
with our arms we point out the position of
time.
We'll all be there, a celebration so rare!
It's the coolest place to be,
a Quimmy bash, for Valena at last,
in the stump of the hollow tree.

They bowed politely to each other, then to Valena, and left, flying back out the open window, fluttering fast towards the forest as there was no time to waste.

"Goodbye," yelled Valena out the window, mesmerized by their visit.

"Me, I'm invited to a party. How exciting," Valena said. She suddenly realized that today was a special day. She quickly ran behind an old lace dressing screen.

"Oh, I have to hurry," she said excitedly, then put on a new purple patchwork lace dress that Rosey and Posey had bought her for a special occasion. She buttoned it up and ran over to look into an old mirror which sat in the centre of her small vanity table. She turned slowly about, looking at herself.

"Well, I can't really see myself in this dismal old mirror, so I'll just imagine my dress looks pretty," she said happily, then sat down on the small round vanity stool covered with her favourite red wool baby blanket and reached for her hair brush.

"Oh, this dirt in my hair will never come out," she complained, brushing her hair into a ponytail. She tied it with a purple ribbon then peered closely at her image in the mirror. Even though the reflection was dull and dimly distorted, Valena could see that her long silver and black-entwined hair still glistened.

"Maybe one day I will be a great hair dresser and I can cut all this dust out of my hair," she commented to herself then put on her boots, which had been sitting under her small stool. She laced them up tightly, jumped up from the stool, and hurried out of the bedroom and down the hall to the staircase, jumping two steps at a time until she waltzed herself right into the kitchen where Posey was making breakfast.

"Good morning," said Posey, giving Valena a big hug.

"Good morning," answered Valena, then waited a second. The smell of freshly baked purpleberry tea biscuits filled the kitchen. The fancy table setting gave it away.

"Happy Birthday, Valena!" Posey cried with excitement. "Today is your sixteenth birthday!"

"Where is Rosey?" asked Valena eagerly.

"She went to pick up your present," replied Posey with a happy teasing smile.

"Give me a little hint," Valena begged.

"Ok…it's…small, and there may be a bow on it."

Valena's eyes opened wide, trying to imagine what it could be.

"You're pulling my leg, Auntie Posey," giggled Valena. Posey giggled too, then handed Valena three porcelain china plates to put at each table setting. She also gave her butter and homemade purpleberry jam from the cooler box. Valena put them on the table then sat down on one of the chairs, fidgeting with excitement as she waited patiently for Rosey to return with her present.

Then Rosey came plodding into the house wearing her dirty rubber gardening boots.

"Good morning. I see some of us don't get up with the birds," she said, exasperated. "Happy Birthday Valena!" Rosey seemed to be in a tizzy, her favourite gardening dress was soiled with a small wet yellow stain.

"Here's your present," she said, holding up a droopy-faced skinny little black dog. "I hope he likes you better then he likes me!"

"Thank you, Rosey!" replied Valena, jumping up to hug her and taking the dog.

She held the ugly black skimpy-haired little beast in her arms.

"Hello, sir, pleased to meet you," Valena said very politely, looking closely at him.

"He can't talk," commented Rosey.

Valena held him close then sat back down and cradled him in the material of her dress between her knees.

"But, we still need to be properly introduced," Valena suggested.

"Of course you do," said Posey.

"But of course," mocked Rosey. She rolled her eyes, looked sideways, then quickly turned and headed right out the door towards the old garden shed.

"Tea, anyone?" called Posey, looking a little disappointed.

"Not now, we are already behind," Rosey yelled back towards the house.

"Oh, well," Posey sighed. "We will have our tea and biscuits just the three of us," Posey said, giving Valena a gentle smile. Then she took the dog from Valena's lap, patted its little head, and put him on the floor beside her.

"I have something for you too!" said Posey, handing Valena a small fancy old glove box. Valena opened it. Inside was a very neatly folded white fine linen hanky. "Unfold it gently," suggested Posey. Inside the pretty hanky, at the very centre of it, was the faint purple imprint of a flower and crumbled petals.

"It's very pretty Aunt Posey, but…what was in it?" she asked, waiting for one of her aunt's strange tales, like the one about the dead Gypsies and how she believed they haunted the forest.

"This gift, my precious," Posey said, tearing up, "was a pretty purple sweet pea that was wrapped up with you that terrible snowy night you came to us, and…well, I…I pressed it into this lovely hanky and saved it for you, all these years."

"Thank you, Posey, I will keep it forever and ever."

"And what do you think of that?" Valena asked the little dog still sitting on the floor looking up at her. "I think you need a name."

"Hmm…I think I'm going to call you…Sir," she said. The dog looked up at her with his big round bulgy brown eyes, amazed at how ghostly white she was.

"Sir, that's a nice name," Posey said, dabbing the corners of her mouth daintily with her cotton serviette.

After breakfast they laughed and played with Valena's new pet for a few minutes then heard a terrible clanging and banging noise coming from outside. It was Aunt Rosey near the old garden shed, having one of her hissy fits.

"Valena!" she screamed loudly.

"Coming!" Valena yelled back, and grabbing Sir she ran as fast as her slight body could go up the cobblestone pathway towards the shed.

When she reached Aunt Rosey she didn't dare question her odd ways. Rosey yanked at the old garden shed door impatiently.

"This stubborn old door!" she yelled. "It won't open!"

"Let me help," Valena said.

She put Sir on the ground a little ways from the door then grasped the rusty door handle and pushed down on the button. The door opened effortlessly. Rosey stepped back and gave Valena an odd look.

"That's strange . . ." said Rosey, spooked.

She then pushed the door open all the way and went inside the shed. Valena followed her, Sir tagged along too.

"It's very dusty in here," Valena said, crinkling up her little nose and sniffing.

"It hasn't been opened for sixteen years," Rosey responded, and looked at the purple scarf and black hooded cloak that hung on the back of the shed door.

"I thought . . . well, actually, Posey and I thought you could clean up the shed and use it as a place to do your gardening. An extra birthday gift," Rosey offered in an underhanded tone.

Valena sneezed from the dust. She parted the cobwebs with the ends of her fingers to make a pathway through to the back of the narrow shed. Rosey choked from the dust then quickly went back outside.

"Enjoy your new gift," she called back into the shed, holding the door open.

"I will come back to see you after the shed is tidied. Try to get it finished before your flower deliveries, which, because you are now sixteen, you will be doing all by yourself," Rosey announced, then let go of the door and it slammed shut.

"Myself?" cried Valena. "All by myself? My own flower deliveries?"

She jumped for joy and giggled with excitement, then rushed to the shed door and pushed it open.

"Thank you, Aunt Rosey!" she called out happily.

Rosey was already halfway back to the cottage but stopped and turned back towards the shed.

"I will come and see how you are doing in a while," she yelled to Valena, then continued on her way.

Valena watched her go. Sir's sharp barking brought her attention back to the shed, he was looking up at her eagerly, wagging his tail.

"Oh, I see…you want to play!" she said, laughing as she waved more cobwebs out of her way and started to explore her very own shed. On a top shelf next to a very dirty cracked window she noticed an old watering can. Valena stepped up on a stool next to a work counter, stretched her arms up, and brought it down.

"Look, Sir," she said to her new friend, offering him a look. The small dog came up cautiously, his ears flattened back on his little head. He gave a timid sniff at the old can and tilted his head sideways, perplexed, then slowly backed away. Then he suddenly sneezed as Valena blew the dust off and it flew everywhere.

"Phew," she said with a grimaced look on her face. The initials M.T. were marked on the can. Hmm…thought Valena, I wonder what that means. Then she noticed an unusual pair of cotton lace gardening gloves sitting on the window ledge.

"Just imagine what's under all this dust, Sir," said Valena.

The dog had found a comfortable spot in a straw basket on the floor and was making himself at home.

"That's okay, Sir. You sleep, while I clean."

Valena bent down to pick up an old straw sun hat that was laying on the floor. As she stood back up she bumped her head on a piece of wood that was sticking out of the wall. In a state of dizziness she noticed a dusty oval mirror hanging crookedly on the wall. She blew the dust particles away, put the hat on her head, then tried to see herself in the mirror.

"Hello, I'm Valena, I'm a florist," she giggled, as she introduced herself to the reflection in the worn glass.

All at once she heard music. The lovely sound of a symphony orchestra was coming from inside the watering can with the M.T. initials. She picked it up and took it over by the window to see if she could get a closer look into the bottom of it. Valena blew into the can and the dust flew right up into her face. She blinked her eyes and opened them wide in disbelief for there, on the bottom of the can, was a group of tiny white fluffy insects.

"Hellooo in there!" she called, and her voice echoed from the watering can.

"Madam, have you any idea to whom you're speaking?" came a tiny voice from inside the bottom of the can.

Valena was stunned. She looked even closer and blew even harder than before to see what was really at the bottom of the can and who or what was talking to her.

"Could you please stop blowing on my orchestra?" said the annoyed insect, in a quick high voice that she could hardly understand. "Allow me to introduce myself. I am the great conductor, Wooley Aphididae, and this is my orchestra of woolly aphids."

"Wooley who?" asked Valena.

"Anyway," Aphididae snapped, disregarding her question as he held up his pin-sized wand in the air.

Valena shook her head and thought, I must be dreaming. She backed away from the old watering can, amazed at the beautiful symphony music that was being played. It got louder and louder. Valena thought maybe

Rosey and Posey might hear it as well. All of a sudden the shed window flew open wide and the hat on Valena's head began to twirl itself around.

"La la la, I am Harriet," sang the hat.

The straw hat flew right off Valena's head and up into the air. It spun around then settled back onto Valena's head magically, turning her around and around, making her dance about the small shed.

A delightful parade from the gardening brigade began as the rake got up and danced with the spade. A mother pot, and her little pots too, spun around to the sound of the flute. The gardening gloves flew onto Valena's hands, magically moving them around to the sound of the band. The fancy gloves introduced themselves.

The right hand said, "I'm Lacey," and the left hand said, "I'm Hastey." They moved really quick like a magicians best trick.

Suddenly, as she danced about the shed, a song came out of Valena's mouth.

What kind of girl am I,
what will my future be.

Will I figure out the tribulations of life,
will I ever really get to know me.
Will I deliver papers of great importance in
life,
or marry a hairdresser and be his wife.
Maybe I'll be an inspector in the crime scene of
life.
I know ... I'll be a seamstress or a poet.
Busy or idle for who knows what I'll be?
For what kind of girl am I?
And what will my future be?
Maybe I'll be a dresser for the king and queen,
or a ferocious lion trainer and make a crowd
scream.
Oh, I don't know what kind of girl I'll be,
but I want to find out,
and I will,
because I'm me!

Valena was dancing faster and faster then suddenly the music stopped. Lacey and Hastey flew off Valena's hands and up into the air. Hastey grabbed a ball of string off the countertop and Lacey scooped up some pretty ribbon. Out the window they magically flew.

Sir had awakened and was watching this marvellous show. He jumped out the window after Lacey and Hastey. Valena ran to the shed door but it wouldn't open. She ran over to the window and saw the gloves working diligently, stringing beautiful flowers together from the garden. They were filling the old wooden flower cart that was sitting outside the garden shed.

Sir tried to catch Lacey but she gave him a swat. Then he ran after Hastey, too swift to get caught. Within minutes, Valena's flower cart was filled to the top with beautiful bouquets of fresh flowers and purple orchid boutonnieres. Valena moved aside as Sir jumped back in through the window, still chasing the gardening gloves, which dropped themselves back on the dusty ledge. The window slammed shut, the string and the bows were back in their places and M.T., the watering can, was now silent, not an aphid in sight. The hat on Valena's head fell back onto the floor. The whole shed was clean. A knock came from outside the door.

"Valena!" called Posey. "Are you still cleaning up?"

Valena felt so dizzy as the spellbinding

experience suddenly ceased. She teetered across to the shed door and pushed it open quickly, almost knocking her two aunts over onto the ground. Rosey looked at her critically.

"Oh dear, Valena, you are more pale than usual. Are you sick?" asked Posey.

"Nothing like good hard work to make a girl strong!" stated Rosey.

Valena was drained and confused. She didn't let on that she had not cleaned the shed herself.

"Poor thing, she's probably suffocating from all the dust," Posey surmised, as the two busybody sisters entered the shed to inspect it.

"It's...spotless!" Posey exclaimed.

Valena looked with puzzlement at them both. Sir was panting and alert. Suddenly a little white cat darted from a dark corner and quickly scampered out of the shed, her fluffy tail flying behind her. In an instant, Sir darted out the door after her, followed by Valena and her two aunts.

"Oh! A cat," cried Posey. "Oh my, oh dear, stop him!"

"Sir! Come here!" Valena yelled. He was gone.

Rosey turned anxiously to look at the flower cart, now filled with beautiful flowers standing ready for delivery.

"Posey and I are proud of you, Valena. Aren't we, Posey?" Rosey offered, with a rare sentiment of praise. "Well, it looks to me like you're all set to go."

"Yes, I think I am," Valena answered, her eyes glistened with eager anticipation as she looked at the beautiful flowers arranged to perfection in the cart.

"I told you she was special," Posey boasted with a broad smile.

Sir appeared from behind the shed, returning from his fruitless pursuit of the little white cat. He went to Valena and looked up at her, begging with his eyes for her to tell the spinsters that she needed him for company on her delivery trip.

"How did you manage to get all this done?" asked Rosey, perplexed.

"You might say...I had a little hand or two, right, Sir?" Valena joked, looking down at the dusty dog. Rosey gave Valena one of her blank stares.

"I'll go fetch Kermack," said Posey. She

stepped across to a small barn and led back an old silver-grey horse whose coat had an eerie shine to it. An old metal chain hung from its neck, on it a medallion that read, KERMACK, and that's what they called him. Posey had found him many years ago, wandering on the outskirts of their field that same cold winter night that Valena had come to live with them. Posey said he had the strangest shine to his coat and looked like he may have belonged to the Gypsies; that he had probably been used to pull their caravans on their travels. Rosey said that Posey's imagination was going to carry her off in her sleep one night.

Rosey instructed Valena that when she made her flower deliveries she should wear the black cloak that was hanging on the back of the shed door. She told her to always keep the cloak hood covered over her dirty hair so that no one would see it. Posey took the purple scarf that had been hanging under the cloak and gently put it around Valena's neck, then she tied a pretty bow to secure the hood on her head.

"There, you look lovely," she said, primping at the scarf.

The two aunts hitched Kermack, the old faithful horse, to the delivery cart.

"Sir is coming with me, isn't he?" asked Valena.

"I don't see why not," Posey answered, "but you must go directly to the castle, deliver the flowers, and come straight home."

"Maybe he'll keep you from getting into trouble," Rosey added, patting Sir's head with a heavy hand and giving him a stern look as if to say stay out of trouble. The dog frowned at this.

"Oh, yes, definitely," Valena agreed eagerly, then bent down to pick up Sir. She dusted him off, then put him up on the bench so he could sit beside her. Then she gave her aunts a big hug each, climbed up into the driver's seat and picked up the reins. Posey's eyes began to fill with tears. Valena snapped the reins gently.

"Let's go, Kerm," she commanded proudly.

The big cob horse started to move his large hairy hooves, pulling the cart forward down the narrow path that led to the road. Valena turned to look back at her aunts and waved goodbye to them. They both waved back. Posey's eyes were now blurred with tears. Rosey handed her a torn lace hanky to wipe them with.

"Thank you, Rosebud," Posey said as she sniffled and dabbed at her eyes.

As the flower delivery cart moved closer to the road, Sir sat tall and proud beside Valena who was still looking back. Flower Petal Cottage and her two aunts got farther and farther away, smaller and smaller, until, when the cart turned a gentle curve, they disappeared altogether. On this early bright autumn morning Valena suddenly realized that for the first time in her life she was on her own, she was responsible for her own destiny. She shivered with excitement and the challenge that she, her loyal horse, Kermack, and her feisty little dog, Sir, were journeying out into the big world all by themselves. With a deep breath of eager youthful confidence, Valena guided the horse onto the road that would lead them to the ancient castle of Zymurgy.

SEVEN

Gypsy Magic

It was a lovely autumn day and Kermack plodded along the rocky road. Valena looked down at her companion, Sir. He was sitting majestically with his snout up, enjoying the cool air and picking up scents that only a dog could smell. The two new friends made their way along the dusty road. Valena noticed a cool breeze gently leading the leaves on the trees into a slow waltz.

"The trees are dressed for fall, Sir," Valena announced.

Sir looked at her, crooked his head to the side, then lay down with his paws hanging over the leather bench. Valena gave the reins a little snap as Kermack sometimes lagged along. Just as they picked up the pace, a tall skinny stranger with wild white hair went galloping by them on a huge black stallion.

As he did he turned his head slyly, saw the purple Gypsy scarf and recalled seeing this girl somewhere before, then he carried on.

This frightened Valena. Dust from the dry ground flew everywhere. Sir choked as Valena slowed down a bit.

"He must be going somewhere very important," Valena said.

"The audacity of that rider to douse my coat in dust," protested Sir, brushing himself off and looking disgusted.

"You can talk?" gasped Valena, shocked.

"As English is, I do," replied Sir.

"Wait until Rosey and Posey hear this!" Valena exclaimed.

"If Rosey and Posey find out I can articulate, they will put me in a circus or something as bad," the dog said.

"I won't say a word," Valena promised.

"Until death do us part?" Sir asked, looking up at her.

"Until what?" said Valena, looking puzzled.

"Just button your lips," said Sir.

"Okay," replied Valena.

I knew she'd get that one, Sir thought to himself.

"Don't worry Sir, you're just a normal dog," giggled Valena.

"Someone should have told my mother that one, the old Picket Pretoff," said Sir sarcastically. "I am a dog of few words and I'd like to keep it that way."

"All right," said Valena.

In the distance Valena could see a pond. Just above it, a small mountain of rock.

The pond was not very big but it was deep. Rosey and Posey had told her that a long time ago a beautiful silver waterfall used to fall from the side of that mountain and filled a bottomless pond with cool fresh water. Now it was just a murky duck pond. But it wasn't just any duck pond, it was the home of a beautiful swan couple, Julia and Henry. Valena had named them when she was a small child. Julia was beautiful, the whitest swan Valena had ever seen and Henry was a black swan, with the shiniest black feathers that ever a black swan had.

"Whoa," said Valena, as she pulled back on Kermack's reins.

Sir thought to himself, did she really need to slow him down?

Valena always stopped to watch the elegant swans floating in the pond and found it unfair that their black and white feathers of romance were soaked by such murky waters.

Starting back up again the jolt of the cart made a small bouquet of flowers topple off the back and roll down to the edge of the pond. Valena got down to pick them up and, as she did, noticed a distorted reflection in the murky water. She reached out her hand and put it into the cold slimy water, then pushed it away. Between the outward ripples she could see her face had no colour. She pulled back her hooded cloak and put her hands on the sides of her hair, touching it gently. Her scalp felt as though it was tingling, her black and silver hair shone vividly in the morning sunlight. Valena slowly got up and turned around to go back to the cart with a look of dismay upon her face.

Sir watched her intensely then raised the bottom of his jaw and pinched his top lip with his lower teeth, realizing Valena had seen herself as peculiar.

"Uh, oh," he whispered. At once he jumped into the back of the cart amongst the flowers, hopping around like he had springs on his feet.

Valena saw him hopping from one end of the cart to the other.

"Phew, I'm getting out of breath," he said to himself, trying as hard as he could to make her laugh so she wouldn't worry about her looks, then he asked himself, why was she so ghostly pale?

Valena walked towards the cart and put the flowers back in their place. As she did, Sir popped his head out from amongst what used to be an organized arrangement of flowers and licked her right on the end of her cute little nose.

"Yuck," shrieked Valena. "Your breath smells like seashells."

Sir grinned.

"Thank you Valena. At least it doesn't smell like that stinky pond water," Sir replied, jumping back onto the front seat, taking his place once more.

Valena laughed and climbed back up onto her cart. Kermack had been sleeping. He enjoyed his job, it could be very satisfying at times.

"Click, click," Valena said as she snapped the leather reins, "away we go." Kermack started to move forward.

"Valena, I have a joke for you," said Sir.

"Okay," said Valena.

"Knock, knock."

"Who's there?"

"You're slower," the dog said.

"You're slower then who?" asked Valena.

"You're slower then Kermack," said Sir with a smirk.

"That's not a joke!" accused Valena

"Oh, yes it is," Sir replied in defence.

Kermack pulled them past the duck pond and they headed along a short pathway.

"Sir, am I strange?" Valena questioned. "I'm so pale and my hair, it's an odd colour. Don't you think so? Everything has a colour except me. What colour am I?"

"You?...You!...Are...a unique colour!" said Sir, in a complimentary fashion.

"I'm unique? That's it! I am a unique colour," she said, as she held her head up with pride.

"Now, put on your hood," said Sir.

"Yes, I have to remember what Rosey

and Posey told me," said Valena. "You're so smart, Sir," she said, as she patted him on his small hairless head.

"Easy," said Sir as he squished up his face. He hated being treated like a little dog.

They began to climb a gnarled pathway. Up ahead Valena could see a beautiful valance of sweet peas hanging down from the tunnel entrance to the giant hollow tree stump. The smell of sweet flowers filled the air. Valena loved this part of the trip. She had been through here many times before with Rosey and Posey but never told them what she was about to tell her new companion. So on the way up, before entering the big tree stump, she told Sir one of the biggest secrets of her life and how this place was the most wonderful place in the whole world.

"Sir…Sir…" Valena said, hesitating. The dogs attention was drawn to her.

"Yes," answered Sir.

"You can never, ever, tell anyone what I'm going to tell you. I have a big secret that I've kept since I was eight years old." Then, Valena spoke quietly.

"One beautiful fall morning I wandered

far from the cottage to play in the woods. Soon after an eerie thunderstorm started and a huge bright purple lightning bolt suddenly hit the ground. I was afraid, so I quickly ran inside this big hollow tree stump to hide. It started getting cold in there like the middle of winter and it began to snow. It was beautiful, I couldn't believe my eyes. Then it turned into an awful blizzard, everything became frozen, I was so cold that I had to get out of there! So I ran, slipped and fell. There I lay, helplessly, on top of something that was frozen, solid and glowing. I looked from side to side and saw my whole body was resting on a frozen bed of sweet peas in the middle of a snowstorm. I didn't move a muscle and was afraid to get up. I swear I saw a ghost! But it was just more frozen sweet peas, on the inside of the big frozen roots of the old hollow stump and they were shaped like a lady, sitting with her hands folded gracefully upon her lap, as though she was waiting for someone. As a frosty wind blew I heard footsteps upon the icy ground, then gathering around me were some kind of little silver stick-like creatures, lots of them, with brightly lit glowing hands and feet that looked like candy, and they talked in high funny voices. I was afraid to speak. I was frightened of them. They came really close to me and tried to help me up, but I somehow got myself up and ran as fast as I could, slipping all the way out of the big hollow tree stump. Back to the cottage I ran, never telling Rosey and Posey what I had seen or heard because they'd never let me out again."

"Ah…huh…glowing hands, candy feet, seen them many times before!" Sir said. Quite an imagination he thought, snickering to himself.

"After that day my curiosity kept me going back and I made friends with the strange creatures. They told me this land they lived on was magical and someone had burnt their village down to the ground, and that same night their old Gypsy queen cast a spell on them which sent them to live up inside this hollow tree stump and become part of a magical plan." Wow, this is getting good, Sir thought. He lay down and stared at Valena.

"They call themselves the Quimmy Boinks and they told me that when I turn sixteen I would become part of a secret plan and my odd hair would become magical. So every once in a while they would pull my silver hair out and put it in a secret hiding place. They also told me that their glowing candy-like hands and feet, called glow plugs, are so bright that they have to put them in dark little bags under their beds at night so they can sleep.

"On another occasion we had an afternoon tea stump party—what a treat! I got to taste one of their sweet, sticky, delicious tree sap hands. When I got to know them better they showed me some old grey stones by the tree stump and, with tears in their eyes, told me that the stones use to be magical and bring people good luck. But since the spell had been cast upon them, the beauty of the stones had lost their magic. Now the Quimmies hide from strangers, for the legend is that after the spell, if anyone were to capture one of these beautiful, delicate creatures, they could take off their hands and feet of candy from their arms and bowed legs and eat them, and it would bring them a lifetime of good luck. They taught me the Quimmy upside down handshake of trust and, depending on the weather conditions, it could be quite a sticky bond of friendship. Sometimes they talked about scary old ghost graves that lay inside old Silver Mountain where the waterfall use to be."

"Ghosts…Graves!" Sir gulped, sat up and wiggled over beside her.

"And their great Gypsy queen's ghost secretly told them to have a special princess party for me on my sixteenth birthday. I'm so excited, I've been waiting all these years for this special day."

Sir stared at Valena. It all sounded so…so…eerie. Then Sir, being a noble dog, thought that if a ghost was going to scare them to death he might as well do his duty and protect them.

"I'll be your prince in shining armour!" Sir spouted.

"Silly, you're my dog!" Valena chirped.

"Prince Dog."

"Noooo…Sir…you're the dog." Sir slouched.

Valena and Sir now entered the big hollow tree stump. Above the entrance, hiding in the pretty flowers, was Wispy Boink a little Quimmy bug who looked like a waif, with dried pinecones that were used as rollers in her frizzy wild green hair. She was giving hand signals to the other bugs, warning them that Valena and Sir were coming into the tree stump.

"She's here, pass it on," she called out.

"Ready, ready," answered Cookie Boink in his bakers hat. His stick-like legs supported the centre of his round cookie-shaped middle and, twirling around, he warned the other Boinks that the birthday girl had arrived.

"Okay! Is every one set? They're coming in," sang Merry Boink, a heavier set grandmother Quimmy who was adjusting a pretty scarf that covered her bald bug head.

As Valena and Sir went under the beautiful hanging sweet peas into the gigantic tree stump, Sir jumped into the back of the cart and hid amongst the flowers. It was very dark and scary inside this place. In Valena's mind it was just part of the magic that lay within this cool damp hollow stump.

Most famous Picket Pretoff breeds have

been known for their bravery, Sir thought, as he shook from fear.

Kermack seemed to know his way through the ancient stump quite well, as though he had been through it a hundred times before.

Appearing suddenly, up inside the top of the hollow tree stump, a show of bright glowing tiny hands and feet displayed the words HAPPY BIRTHDAY.

"Happy Birthday, Happy Birthday," screamed the hidden high little voices.

Many coloured lights began to shine throughout the darkness from the inside of the tree stump. Valena stopped Kermack and got down excitedly from the cart. Her pale face took on the many pretty colours as they glowed brightly.

"Surprise!" they screamed from up above.

"Oh, goodness, what a wonderful surprise," Valena said, her eyes sparkled.

Sir cautiously poked his head up above the flowers in the cart to see who she was talking to. He blinked a few times, adjusted his eyes, and looked about the place.

"Wow! A party!" Sir spoke childishly, then suddenly put on a poker face. Looking over at Valena he noticed that her face now looked like a well used page from a child's colouring book.

"And she thought she looked strange before," he snickered to himself.

The pretty lights sparkled around the vines and sweet peas, these little creatures were sharing Valena's birthday with her. Higher up inside the darkness of the tree stump were their brightly lit, diamond-shaped stained glass houses, each the size of a fully bloomed sunflower. Shiny silver vines hung from the bottom of their small houses. They came half way down the vines, greeting Valena, their soft delicate wings fluttering about gracefully.

"Hello, everyone," said Valena.

"Valena, psst, Valena," called Sir, eyes bulging in disbelief.

"Don't be afraid," Valena giggled. "They're my friends."

"Real ones?"

"Like family," said Valena, looking at them fondly.

"Oh, dear," Sir replied. "Ahem," he cleared his throat, "yes...well then...hello."

"I'm...still here?" he questioned, pinching himself.

"Of course you are," giggled Valena.

"Yes...I am...here. Think of all the nice families I could have gone to," he sulked. Sir stared at the odd little creatures and they in turn stared back. I'll be darned, Sir thought, Valena was not kidding about their odd little silver stick-like bodies and their skinny, slightly bowed legs, and upon their backs were beautiful, delicate, soft grey pussy willow wings.

"Hi, Valena," called Wispy Boink. The tiny silver bug's pussy willow wings were tattered and spread far apart, but they helped hold up a short, delicate, funny-looking red dress.

"Hello, Wispy," replied Valena, "what a nice surprise." Then Wispy Boink got all nervous and giggled so hard that her bright pink glow plugs fell right down onto the ground. Looking embarrassed, she climbed down quickly and put them back on.

"We are all excited for your special princess party!" said Wispy Boink.

"She's right on time!" said Tic Boink.

"Any time might be the right time in the big hollow stump!" said Toc.

"I baked you my special inside-out cake!" said Cookie Boink, tipping his oversized puffy bakers hat, then brushing cake batter from his baggy purple patchwork apron.

"Cake," said Sir, licking his lips, he'd once again risen to the scene after hearing what Cookie Boink had said.

Then an old voice piped up from inside the tree trunk. It was old Bossy Boink. He appeared from behind a big giant root and stood in the shadows of the ancient tree stump. He was a miniature Quimmy and the oldest one in the stump. He could yell loud but being so small you could hardly hear him. He had a pin-sized eagle tooth cane, it helped him keep his balance as he was unsteady on his worn, silver bug-sized spike leg. His tiny overalls held up his small sagging old Quimmy wings the best they could. He pulled a fresh green leaf from his pocket and wiped it across his bug head leaving a green streak.

"Not as organized as I used to be," said old Bossy Boink.

"Oh! LOOK OUT HERE! I'm bringing the cake down," cried Cookie Boink.

Cookie Boink boinked his way across some vines and with a big bang he dropped the whole cake down onto the ground.

"Ugh...sorry," he said.

Valena tried not to laugh at him but he seemed kind of silly sometimes.

"If I didn't know better, I would claim this situation of yours a national disaster," commented Sir, once again popping his head out from amongst the flowers.

Then Merry Boink appeared on her vine, nearly snapping it with her weight. She winked at Valena with her big soft brown and yellow bug eyes.

"You're all so busy," said Valena.

"We have something special for you," Merry Boink said. All the Quimmies stuck their candy-like hands together and, while hanging upside down on their pretty vines by their little bright glowing feet, they formed a friendly circle just a few feet above Valena's head and sang in Quimmy style.

With a Gypsy spell we were sent here to live,
and our friend you've truly been.
And spared from the fire, what we truly desire,
is to help our princess, become queen.
And so at last we've finished your gift,
it's magical you see.
It will protect your life and make you strong,
and bring you back to us where you belong.

Just then the most beautiful soft purple-coloured light gleamed throughout the tree trunk. Coming slowly down from the highest roots of the tree and through the sweet peas was a magnificent stained glass Quimmy mansion, the size of a baby bassinet, which hung from a thick pretty silver and purple vine with silver bows tied to it. From it, colourful sparks flew in every direction. On the end of it was a small basket with Valena's birthday present inside. As the Quimmies' vines started to lower onto the ground, they helped direct the gift towards Valena.

Suddenly ten little Boinks fluttered about as they landed one of the most beautiful gifts they had ever created right into Valena's hands. The gift was wrapped in a blanket of soft pussy willow Quimmy wings. Everyone stood still as colours sparkled around the ground throughout the big tree stump.

"It's for you, our princess," said Merry Boink, folding her hands. Tears were in her eyes.

Valena could feel the softness of the folded pussy willows wings. She couldn't believe her eyes, it was all like a beautiful dream.

"Go ahead, unwrap it," giggled Wispy Boink.

Merry Boink motioned her to silence with a stare.

All the Quimmies stood in silence, waiting for their princess to open her gift.

Valena slowly opened the delicate Quimmy wings. She looked at the gift, it was the most beautiful thing she had ever seen, a strangely enchanting mask.

"It's magically strong!" called out Wispy Boink.

"Try it on, try it on," said Cookie Boink.

"With romantic black and white swan feathers, too!" said Wispy Boink, batting her long wispy eyelashes. "We all pitched in and made it!"

Sixteen long years it took the Quimmy Boinks to artfully create Valena's beautiful mask, with its powerful strong hair sewn all around and in-between the soft feathers.

"It's so beautiful," Valena said, "thank you." She smiled, looking around at her little friends.

At that, she ran over to her cart and hid her gift under a board beneath the flowers.

All the Quimmies clapped their glow plugs and cheered after Valena thanked them for the wonderful surprise, then she climbed back up onto her cart. Once again Kermack found himself being awakened from another peaceful sleep.

Snap went the reins.

"Giddy up," Valena called.

"Giddy up," Sir mocked. "Miracles never cease to happen around here," said Sir, still feeling a little uneasy about the whole situation.

Kermack picked up the pace and they moved toward the end of the tunnel of the old tree stump, then he slowed down again just enough so that Valena and Sir, who was poking his little head out from the flowers, could see old Bossy Boink heading for a large root, balancing on his small silver spike leg. He had a view of all the Quimmies throughout the big tree trunk. He stood very still, leaning on his eagle tooth cane. Valena waited for him to raise the tooth in the air as he always did. He gave this motion; it seemed to say I will see you again sometime. Then Kermack plodded slowly toward the exit of the hollow tree stump.

EIGHT

The Forest

After leaving the darkness of the big hollow stump, Valena, Kermack and Sir squinted as the bright sunlight shone down upon them.

"What a glorious morning," Sir piped up. "Warm sunshine, good for the bones," he commented as he stretched his skinny legs, glad to be out of that tree stump!

Valena looked at Sir, she tried to hold in her laughter but it burst right out.

"Aww Sir," said Valena, "you look so sweet with your ears all done up in sweet peas."

Sir glared at Valena like she was an enemy.

Each of Sir's ears had a fresh flower pushed into it, pink at that. Sir spat out a sour flower from his mouth. The other two he quickly removed with a shake of his noble little head. He was not amused.

"Trivial inane comedy," he muttered. "Outright dandish!" This was a cuss word he made up and said when he was embarrassed. Valena continued to giggle. "Pure sheer dandish," he said again, and stuck his snout high in the air and looked into the distance.

Sir was now shivering and had had it up to his neck with the likes of Valena's wild imagination. He pondered his thoughts as he tried to enjoy the warming sunshine on his chilled body. A cool breeze was starting to become part of their day. Kermack's silver mane was flowing in the breeze, then a gust filled Valena's hooded cloak and blew it off her head. Her shiny silver and black hair glistened as the sun danced upon her head.

Sir was still minding his own business and enjoying the scenery as Valena chit-chatted away.

"Sir, one night I had a dream that I lived in a beautiful castle," she said. Her hair came loose from the bow and wrestled with the wind.

"I suppose that would be a nice place to live," said Sir. "Was I in the dream with you by any chance?" he added hopefully.

"Look, Sir! Up ahead!" Valena called out excitedly. "The forest!"

"They always change the subject on me," Sir said hopelessly.

As they travelled down a narrow path towards the big trees, Sir became sceptical about Valena's reasoning. Even though she'd travelled with Rosey and Posey to the castle many times, after the Quimmy party in the tree stump he couldn't help but feel that there was something eerie about this young girl.

Now, Rosey and Posey also felt something was eerie about Valena, from the first minute they saw her that snowy winter night. She was strange looking. Being apprehensive, they'd waited many months to hear of any speculation on the abandoned baby. No word nor gossip came their way and so the spinster twins kept her, loved her, and covered her hair in the company of strangers. They hoped that no one would see her as weird, take her away or harm her. Compelled to make up a terrible lie, they told everybody, who was anybody, even Valena, that she'd been left in their care by a distraught distant cousin who'd already had too many children to raise. They never talked about that night again and were often sickened by their lie.

Why, even to this day the aged spinster twins worried that someone might identify her, and rightfully so, for earlier that day, when Sir and Valena had been travelling to the pond, the mysterious stranger that had charged by them on horseback had remembered seeing Valena when she was younger but couldn't remember where. That stranger was none other than the infamous Tainted Knight, Horrible Horribin.

Long before Valena and Sir had reached the pond, Horrible had gone bolting fearlessly through the darkness of the big hollow tree stump and, coming out the other side where the Gypsy village use to be, he stopped, dismounted his large horse, then tied him to a tree and looked around, still dumbfounded about where the Gypsy village had gone to. Here he usually pined for his losses, but today he thought back to the flower cart, the runty mutt, and the girl who had been wearing a hooded black cloak with a purple scarf. Suddenly an alarm went off in his head, that scarf is only worn by the Gypsy queens of Ecae, old Horrible remembered. Then, familiar greedy evil thoughts began to meddle with his mind.

"Jittery! Jumpin' Gypsies!…I think I smell titanium brewing!" Horrible stated.

"One Gypsy, two Gypsy, three Gypsy four, one less Gypsy won't matter anymore!" he chanted.

And so that evil knight hunkered down behind some purpleberry bushes and, seeing them, remembered his dead brother Isaac had told him a strange story of how the Gypsies used these raw berries like truth serum on dishonest members of their own village and if anyone but an Ecae Gypsy ate them, Mipsie ghosts would come from deep in the forest to haunt them and scare them half to death. Suddenly the despicable old tyrant got an idea, a sickly awful idea. When the young girl shows up he'll pose as a crippled old Gypsy man selling berries and pretend to be sad when she doesn't buy any. He will offer her a taste for free. Then, if in fact she was a real Gypsy, the moment of truth will prevail.

"Finally…I will know all the Gypsies secrets," Horrible laughed out loud and made a fist, clenching it tight and holding it over his head in a victorious fashion. Where had everything been hidden for all these years, he wondered to himself. "Then, after the girl tells me all the secrets, I'll kill her and it will all be mine."

He pulled his heavy metal sword from its sheath and pricked his bony thumb on the end of it, making sure it was sharp, then, picking some of the purpleberries, he put them on the ground in front of him. He flared his large hairy nostrils and breathed in the cool morning air as if it only belonged to him, then he waited for the girl and the dog.

Now old Horrible had been crouching quite a while and was getting stiff and impatient. He stood up to stretch and, stepping forward, he slipped on the pile of plump purpleberries and hit the side of his mouth hard on a sharp grey slate of rock that was sticking up out of the ground. He slowly stood back up, cursing. He brushed off the squashed purpleberries that stained the right thigh of his pant leg and then, wiping his lips with the back of the same hand, he noticed he was bleeding and some of the purpleberry juice had gotten on his lips. Licking it off, it had a sour taste. Sliding his tongue along his top teeth he felt his left front tooth had been knocked out so, ripping a piece of his shirt-tail off, he pressed it into the spot where the tooth had been to stop the bleeding.

Horrible looked around the ground for his tooth, he ruffled the front of his shirt to see if it had somehow caught in there, he was now in pain and tired. He'd been busy all morning near and far collecting valuables and money from people in nearby villages and towns in exchange for numbered metal tags. The tags were the tickets to get into the annual Hair Ball that was being celebrated this evening in his town, called Metalville, where he was the mayor. Every fall he held this event in a lifelong hope of finding the special girl—she had to be an authentic Gypsy princess—so he could get a lead to where the titanium had gone, and the girl with the purple scarf, he figured, had come to him as a bit of luck. A mere missing tooth wasn't going to stop his initial plan.

After the shock had worn off, Horrible adjusted the blood-stained shirttail in his mouth and recalled wiping his berry stained hand across it, his lips tasted awful and his tongue bitter. The inside of his mouth started to pucker, he started to feel light-headed, giddy and intoxicated, then he started laughing to himself, amused by what his fancy free-spirited brother Isaac had told him about the purpleberries. Becoming more and more silly, he started to make fun of Isaac and his belief in the crazy Gypsy stories.

"Well...if I'm not scared half to death," he held his pointer finger behind his ear, pretending to hear a scary Mipsie ghost coming for him, "what will I say? What will I do?" He rolled his eyeballs up into his head and laughed out loud, then waited a minute. "Just as I suspected, nothing hair-raising here," he said, as he looked back over his shoulder. He began to notice a weird taste on the roof of his mouth, he spat on the ground, his tongue felt like it was on fire, his mouth tasted like metal. He put the fingernail of his bony wrinkled old index finger inside his mouth to scrape it and, pulling it back out, it had a gummy sooty tar-like substance stuck to it. He was sickened by this. He spat and spat as the black gummy soot drooled out from his mouth.

Sickly, Horrible gasped for air, it was as though he had inhaled the fumes from a big fire. He choked and coughed, his eyes bulged out of his head, he became confused as to where he was, his mind slid into a hallucinogenic state, he felt like he was under a spell and began to stagger deep into the forest where he saw potholes with small mounds of earth beside them that shimmered as steam rose from them. All around him was the smell of molten metal. As he walked on he suddenly halted in his steps for rising just twenty feet in front of him was an eerie olive green haze with the most beautiful fifty-foot shiny titanium tree appearing from it, like a ship in the fog. This couldn't be, Horrible thought. His gummy soot-tasting mouth soon became clean and he started to feel better, like he was young again.

"It's happened!" Horrible cried. "I've finally discovered the secret to where the titanium is, it's a tree that supplies it!" He jumped around like a fool as it was far beyond his imagination then, looking at the tree, he noticed it had many hand-sized glowing titanium decorations dangling from the ends of its branches, even right up to the very top of the tree. Horrible ran over to it like a child and admired the decorations, all of them resembling war. He reached out his right hand and took the ornament of a knight on horseback off the tree, then screamed at the top of his lungs in pain as it had burnt his fingers. He threw it away onto the steamy shimmering ground. As Horrible stared at it, with a brittle sound, the ornament cracked open and a real live version of itself emerged. Horrible moved back out of the way as a fully-clad evil titanium knight sat upon a titanium horse. It's pin-ball sized steel eyes were aglow, red steam came forcefully from the mean looking horse's flared nostrils as it fired its steel eyes—from its eye sockets, the steel eyes multiplied and shot out like a BB gun at the base of the beautiful titanium tree, leaving a dangerous steel ball carpet all around the ground. Then a horrendous sound of metal banging on metal rang throughout the forest and the tree snapped at the base, the metal roots ripped right up out from beneath the shimmering ground. Horrible watched and moved away, frightened, as the tree fell to the ground with a big creaky clanging noise. All of the ornaments fell off and broke open, emerging from twelve of them were more evil fully-clad titanium knights. Sitting majestically upon their horses they formed a line, side by side then, last of all, they were joined by the knight on the horse that had shot the tree to the ground. Horrible was amazed. They turned their full attention on him as though he were their king; his army, waiting in anticipation to be led into a bloody battle, their horses stirring as their swords and shields were raised high.

Then all at once the ground started to shake and rising magically from the earth were titanium letters the size of graveyard headstones that stuck up crookedly and read—Tainted Knight. Horrible was in a cold sweat even though it seemed a victorious moment for him, then, with a great loud cracking sound, the big titanium tree split right in half and opened like a book. Rising from it came an eerie royal red haze that floated mystically high into the sky and appearing from within it was a mighty titanium castle with towers that painted themselves up into the sky, upon their peaks were flags crested with 'T K' and a silhouette of Horrible's head behind the lettering. The flags were raised high, indicating the beginning of a big battle. As heavy titanium doors opened into the castle the great and infamous King Horrible entered his palace and majestically took his place on his throne.

"At last! My kingdom!" Horrible cried. "My...castle..." He felt a heavy titanium sword hanging from his hip, while a Goth-like heavy titanium crown with blood red jewels magically appeared upon his head. He became fully clothed in titanium, from his robe down to the tip of his knight boots, and he adjusted the sides of his cape just so with his bony hands whose fingers were garnished with all sorts of titanium rings. He sat arrogantly on his titanium throne.

"Now, I am the ruler of this land," Horrible said, and he gloated over the fact that he was finally king and that all the titanium he could ever wish for was right in the palm of his hands. He had it all and all was his, in his glory he spoke and was in full command of his empire.

I'm a man of war, you can plainly see,
a king in charge of an army at large,
and good I'll never be.
I don't make amends to those I hurt,
and play dirty, not fair, you see.
I don't dance or sing or do happy things,
I only want what titanium brings.

"Power and wealth is what I desire, for it I would kill the Gypsy queen, even the princess." Horrible was beginning to feel weak and didn't realize what he was saying as he sat on his mighty throne inside the courtyard of the castle. He looked around and saw a huge dark green ghostly haze forming around the castle walls, it floated up and took the towers, castle walls, and everything around it high up into the sky until it all disappeared, leaving Horrible sitting on his throne alone in the forest. Just when Horrible had had enough, the forest treetops magically lit on fire, their wooden trunks melted like hot wax down all over the ground. Horrible lifted up his feet and as he did a wild wind struck the forest and blew the wax away like it was whipped cream. Getting stronger and stronger the wind blew the great Tainted Knight around and around in circles. Horrible hung on to his throne tightly and was scared half to death. He felt as though he had to jump right out of his own body to save himself. Then the wind suddenly stopped and left him facing the back of Silver Mountain. Horrible was dizzy and tried to focus on where he was. What a relief, he thought to himself, but as he went to get off his throne, it started to hover off the ground. Ten feet up it dumped him right onto the forest floor and disappeared into thin air. Horrible was a mess. Sitting on the ground he looked up at the mountain, which had taken on the image of the distorted ghostly face of old dying Teaspill; the powerful Gypsy queen looked down at him in vengeance. Horrible froze. The dead Gypsy queen's scary face turned into oozing, bubbling molten titanium which began to overflow and run down the mountainside, flooding the forest where Horrible sat with nowhere to go.

Horrible screamed in terror and lay on his side. Crunching himself into a ball, he closed his eyes and covered his head with his arms. He couldn't believe he was going to drown in titanium and was terrified for he never learned to swim. With his eyes squeezed tightly closed he plugged his nose, his hand trembling. He was going to die.

Then silence came, along with the sweet chirp of a wild bird. Horrible slowly raised his head and looked around fearfully, he only saw the mounds of earth with their freshly grown grass upon them. Everything was back to normal. He got up unsteadily and, with the tale of his shirt still in his mouth, he marched angrily back over to the purpleberry bushes and cursed away, slashing them to pieces with his sharp silver sword.

"Tricks! Sneaky Gypsy bunko! That's what this is!" Horrible yelled in anger. "THAT'S IT, IT'S PAYBACK TIME." Horrible had all he could stand. "Horrible never gets what Horrible wants—my titanium!" Then he pulled back his big heavy sword and jabbed it deep into what was left of the purpleberry bushes. Pulling it back out, a ball of thistles the size of a softball was stuck to the end of it. Holding it up in the air he jerked his shoulders about while screaming and having a childish temper tantrum, now driven to insanity.

"Stupid...Gypsies. Ah!" he yelled loudly, his voice echoing through the trees.

With a huge sigh Horrible pulled out the soggy bloodstained shirttail from his mouth and threw it on the ground. He realized he had lost track of time and should have been back at his castle by now, he had to reconsider his plans.

"I will render my prize another way," he said, as he looked down at the autumn leaves beginning to cover the mounds of earth, where, years before, he had made Shway dig deep holes, trying to find the titanium. They never succeeded.

Horrible looked around, discouraged, then walked back over to his horse who he'd named Danger, and talked to the nervous animal who had been waiting for too long.

"It's not for you," Horrible said tiredly, still holding his heavy sword with the thistle ball pointing at the horse. He looked at it and slid the prickly ball off the sword into the leather pouch on the horse's saddle. Then he gurgled out a laugh, he thought it would be funny to take it back and give it to Shway to play with. Horrible got back up onto his horse but, before he left, a past familiar feeling of rejection entered his mind. Teaspill should have been mine he thought. Then the Tainted Knight furrowed his brow tightly, his dilated pupils took on the shape of broken hearts. He clenched his teeth and, with his head shaking, he tried to deny the grief, but his mind only became immersed in anger, not understanding his unfair life.

"I AM the great Tainted Knight! A fool you've made of me!" he bellowed, then he kicked his horse hard in the girth, pounded his fist into the air and took off like a wild man through the forest, homeward-bound to his castle to think of another horrible plan and brag of his new find. He wouldn't waste any more time here and knew by the chain of events that something big and crazy was about to happen.

"One must be careful, these things take time," he lectured to himself, realizing this was not a one man job. "I don't want to lose my head over this!" Then his lips drew into a crooked smirk and he suddenly bellowed the laugh of a crazy man and etched another devious plan into his crazy mind.

Arriving back at the old creepy rusty castle, Horrible got down from his horse, tied him to a tree at the bottom by the old lift, then jabbed his sword hard inside the pouch on the horse's saddle and brought out the prickly thistle ball on the end of it. He headed for the old creaky oxidized lift and when he got to the top he noticed Shway had left the big metal doors into the castle open. Horrible tried to be quiet so he could see what Shway was up to and often wondered if he might let the crazy Gypsy go because he was so absent-minded. As Horrible entered the room he found the giant lazy lumpus sound asleep, his snoring bounced loudly off the metal walls and with his not so fine watchman skills, he wasn't guarding Garth.

Now sixteen years had passed and Garth was still locked, chained and imprisoned in his own caravan. After Horrible and Shway had kidnapped him they removed all of his belongings. Horrible went through them and made sure that there weren't any hidden special Gypsy jewellery, maps or clues to where the titanium may have been kept. Garth knew Horrible may have wrecked his caravan but he could never destroy the home that lay within his heart and he hoped that one day he might be free again. When Horrible went on outings Shway would sometimes come up to the window and talk to the lonely Gypsy man; he wondered why he couldn't speak, but fear kept the dunce giant from developing any kind of relationship with him.

Malnutrition now plagued the rapidly ageing Gypsy man and only a few things were left in the caravan for him—a small wooden stool, a dirty old pillow, and a prickly old horse blanket which Garth would kick around when he was mad because he was allergic to it. He had developed an arthritic condition from sleeping on the hard wooden floor for so many years. Inside Garth's caravan were large hollow spaces at both ends where Horrible and Shway had ripped out Garth and Isa's bed from one end and a burnt purple velvet bench from the other. This made

Garth feel lonelier than ever and tonight he would work long hours in Metalville at the Hair Ball. Every year he hoped that someone would recognize him and free him, but it never happened so he'd given up hope. Garth liked seeing all the costumes at the ball but didn't like how he was made fun of by the unruly guests who, later in the evening as the state of affairs progressed, would make rude remarks and toss goblets of refreshments at him. Not being given his meal until the next evening, Shway, like a child, would sneak him a few morsels and if caught would lie and say he was taking them for his horse.

Garth had heard Horrible come up the lift and march into the room, his knight boots echoed like a drum as he crossed over the metal floor. He grabbed his sword-handled cane off a nearby metal table to support his body as he was out of breath and tired. Garth got up and peered through the crack in the caravan window and tried to see as much as he could of what the old tyrant was doing. He saw he had a thistle ball on the end of his sword. Garth remembered when the Gypsies would use them back in his village around the purpleberry bushes, to keep the birds and animals from eating the berries.

Garth lost sight of Horrible, but he'd looked unusually pale and seemed more out of breath than usual. Horrible was headed in Shway's direction.

Reaching Shway's bedside Horrible held out his big sword with the thistle ball on the end of it and planted it right onto Shway's rear-end. Garth heard the giant man yell, "YOOOOOUCH," then land both giant-sized bare feet onto the metal floor.

"I...AM...your personal wakeup call. I've returned! Happy!" Horrible announced. Shway stood on the opposite side of his bed from Horrible. Teetering, he shook his dozy head and rubbed his rear-end while trying to see what Horrible had poked him with. Then Horrible banged his sword down onto Shway's bed and the ball of thistles bounced off. As stupid as he was, Shway caught it, then threw it above his bed and yelled loudly.

"Oweeeee!" He licked all his fingers in one fell swoop and was now officially awake as the prickly ball fell down and poked itself into his pillow, scattering all over the special blanket that he'd named Softy. He knew that he would have to remove the thistles from Softy later and stood trembling, knowing they were stuck in him. The giant man was befuddled, he hadn't seen Horrible this excited in years.

"And the winner is!" Horrible yelled. "The king! The queen! And, of course, the ACE! I am the happiest man alive, what a find, what a find, pay attention! You lazy idiot, we are back in business, and if…" he stated, "my memory serves me correctly, I love to engage in a battle with an unarmed Gypsy." He laughed. "A coincidence if it were, while I was out and about I found someone very pre…cious. Ewee…Did I say that? YUCK!"

Then Horrible turned, glared at Garth, and walked towards his caravan.

Garth moved back a bit from the crack in the window but could still see Horrible's body strutting back and forth in front of it like an arrogant lunatic.

"Your people are a great mystery, aren't they Gypsy man?" Horrible needled. "And…oh, but of course…you can't talk…pity! Fate says, this may be one of the luckiest days of your life, Horrible!" he boasted to himself.

Garth listened to Horrible carry on like an idiot, but this time something seemed different, Horrible seemed edgy and afraid of something.

Garth, being a simple man, had only one wish—to be back in his peaceful village, to hold his wife, Isa, again, and to kiss the child he had never known. But day after day he suffered from mental anguish and physical scars from having his neck in a metal collar and his wrists and ankles bound in heavy metal cuffs that Shway had made and Horrible had put on him.

Chained to Horrible's horse, Garth was taken into town every day. When he got there Shway and Horrible would take him up into the tower and feed a big main chain through metal loops that were attached to his metal collar and cuffs, this would secure Garth to the mechanism up in the big tower so he could open, close, and maintain the giant gates of the town of Metalville. A dangerous job, with just enough chain so that if he fell he would go down in between the big doors and be crushed, or hang himself with the big heavy rusted chain that kept him from escaping.

But Garth had a plan of his own. Every day he would take the same link and let it bang in the opening gate, hoping that one day the stress would break it off. Then he could get out of the terrible situation he was in. The people of the town called him the Gatemaster. Horrible had taught them to be afraid of him and every day after a long hard day of work, Garth was taken back to the evil castle of the Tainted Knight and given a small amount of water and a stingy meal, then chained back inside his caravan and guarded with no chance for freedom.

Horrible walked slowly, taking long strides in front of Garth's caravan. He was agitated, tapping his cane on the floor. He paced back and forth, putting his head in the air, displaying dominance, then he walked over to the window and he peered in through the small crack.

"Talk, Gypsy," demanded Horrible. "You might as well, because...an Ecae Gypsy has reared her beautiful Gypsy head and she wears the scarf of the Gypsy queens," he taunted Garth.

Garth's mind raced as he kept an eye on Horrible. Had he had a baby girl? Where had Isa and his daughter been for all these years?

"When I was a young man," Horrible explained, "I learned about your absurd customs, how the Gypsy queens of your village made magical jewellery with powers far beyond a man's dreams, and if this is true, I will find out! Answer me!" Horrible waited for Garth to respond. "Still won't talk? Fine! How sad for you! Putting a pretty young thing in such jeopardy," Horrible yelled.

If only I could talk, Garth thought to himself. But the ancient Gypsy ghost queen's curse still plagued Garth, he hadn't spoken in sixteen years. He suffered from terrible heartache and loneliness. He often wondered who had survived the fire in the Gypsy village. Past memories of his wife still pained him but, as time went on, the vivid memory of her beautiful face began to fade. Garth would often lay awake late at night and try hard to recall their life together—her friendly smile, her gentle touch which warmed his heart. He often felt foolish for the thought, but what kept him going was that one day he may see her again and the love he had for his Gypsy girl would never die.

When Horrible talked, Garth never showed any emotion for he knew what Horrible was all about after all these years, and often wondered what had happened in his life to harden his heart and create so much bitterness toward the Gypsy people. Garth wanted to escape and help the girl so Horrible wouldn't hurt her, but what Horrible was saying was more than anything Garth could have ever wished for. This sounded like it might be his daughter. He hoped she was going to be as brave and crafty as the old woman whose scarf she wore.

Garth peered at his captor through the small crack in the window, knowing he was helpless. He moved away from the window back into one corner of the caravan as Horrible roared loudly, "WHERE'S…THE…HEIRLOOM! Well, I guess the beautiful young Gypsy girl will tell me…herself! I'm finished with you!" Horrible sneered, "Let's take this mindless

Gypsy to town and carry on! Shway, I have a plan," he said in a giddy, devilish manner, turning away from the caravan.

"We have an enquiry to make, a fact finding mission you might say, of a sweet young sixteen-year-old Gypsy girl."

"Ah, huh, I get it!" Shway said, tapping his pointer finger on his temple. "We have to find a nice Gypsy girl?" Horrible glared at him. Suddenly Shway grabbed Horrible's cane and jabbed himself in the ribs.

"Give me that!" Horrible yelled, snatching the cane back. "Get! ... The horses ready. Or you'll be working alongside the Gatemaster at the Hair Ball tonight, and oh ... what a fine Hair Ball it's going to be this time around!" Horrible insinuated.

Off into the forest Horrible and Shway rode, first taking Garth to the town, then carrying on with their leather bag full of metal scraps and tools to design a hair salon to trick the lovely young Gypsy maiden and her small companion, and find out through other tactics if she was truly an authentic Gypsy princess.

Meanwhile, as the day was moving along,

Valena and Sir were slowly working their way along a rather rocky path through the big trees in the forest and, being Valena's first time by herself, she hoped she was on the right pathway. For some reason it looked different from the last time she went with her aunts. A cool wind blew across them and Sir decided maybe it was time to join Valena up front, upon a blanket that lay on the leather bench.

Magnificent grey and silver clouds swept overhead. They skimmed along the tree tops making shadows that slid throughout the forest.

Valena had been taught to take this part of her trip very seriously. Sir moved in closer to Valena. She warned him not to let the forest bend his imagination the wrong way. Valena whispered to Sir in a haunting voice. He could feel her warm breath on his head.

"Rosey and Posey told me a story when I was a little girl, that a long time ago in the depths of this forest, a beautiful Gypsy queen died a gruesome death and if you listen close enough on a windy day, you can hear her ghost crying for her Gypsy king who waits

for her to return to the depths of the forest—
BOO!" belted Valena.

Sir's heart jumped inside his hairless body.

"I don't like you! I don't know why I don't
like you," he said, ticked off. "I change my
mind, I mean…I do like you but, just not at
this moment," he looked about nervously.

"Oh, Sir, there are no such things as ghosts,
I think," ventured Valena, doubting herself,
staring off into the trees. She snapped the
reins and Kermack picked up his pace. "My
hair is so messy from the wind." She tried
to put her hood back on. Valena could see
something up ahead on the roadside. "Look,
Sir, what's that?"

Anything's possible now, thought Sir.

There on the roadside was a sign that read
HAIR DOCTOR: Hairologist Dr. Snipper
Lopper Bottom.

Valena steered her cart towards the side
of the road where a junk scrap metal structure had been built to look like a hair salon to
trick the young girl.

Shway was disguised as Dr. Snipper Lopper Bottom. An artistic fellow, he wore a
pink and lime green striped shirt and a pair

of hot pink tights, and on his wide feet were rusted metal boots. His hair was scooped up at the sides into a skimpy broccoli shaped pony tail that sat on the top of his head to hide his baldness.

Horrible had changed his ripped shirt and was wearing a pleated worn dress shirt, the sleeves were held onto his skinny arms by metal arm bands. His black riding pants pinched his waist and the legs were tucked into heavy metal knee-high knight's boots. The two men had been waiting with vengeance in mind for sweet Valena and her little dog.

Valena stopped her cart on the side of the road, then jumped down to read the sign.

"Sir, I can get all this dirt cut out of my hair right here," Valena said eagerly.

"I suppose," said Sir. His sixth sense could smell something odd about these two men.

They stood beside a metal booth. "I do the talking, you do the cutting, got it?" Horrible ordered Shway under his breath.

"Kind of," answered Shway, looking blankly at Horrible.

Behind the booth was a very odd looking chair that sat very high up in the air. It was made of scrap metal pieces and had very sharp jagged arm rests with no cushion on the seat. The footrest had metal knight boots to insert your feet into while getting your hair done. Upon a tray beside the booth were medieval haircutting tools. A sinister hair salon if ever there was one. Valena and Sir started to approach the men.

"Hello, what a lovely purple scarf you're wearing," Horrible greeted her, as he glared sideways at Shway with one of his eyebrows raised. "And what can we do for the lovely prin—I mean, lovely lady today?" he offered in a sickly, sugary manner.

"Well," Valena said sweetly, "I have this hair, it's been dirty all my life and Rosey and Posey could never get it clean."

Sir was looking at Valena, trying to get her attention, his eyes were protruding out of his small skull. He was shaking his head back and forth very slowly as a warning that she shouldn't be telling complete strangers about her hair.

"Oh, how sad," Horrible said. "Poor Rosey and Posey, poor you."

"Can you help me?" Valena said naively,

looking at the two men.

After pricking his fingers on the thistle ball earlier that day, Shway had bandaged most of his fingers with pieces of dirty old rags. He'd tied them neatly into tight little bows on the ends of his tender red fingertips, cutting off the circulation. He was now playing finger puppets with them and laughing to himself as Horrible talked with Valena. Shway carried on and randomly removed each individual bow and kissed each sore inflamed fingertip, dropping each rag to the ground. His fingers were far too sore to work.

"Oh, I'm terribly sorry," he said, blowing on his fingertips, "we're all booked up this afternoon and we couldn't possibly fit you i...n." Horrible shoved Shway out of the way.

"Come. Sit, please!" Horrible said, as he motioned Valena to the cold metal chair with one of his bony hands, ignoring Shway's childish behaviour.

"Are you sure you can cut all this dirt out of my hair?" asked Valena.

"Well..." Shway tried to answer gently, but Horrible leaned on Shway's foot with the end of his cane.

"Shway would love to cut your hair, wouldn't you Shway? And right now," Horrible commanded. "Are you attending the Hair Ball this evening? It's such a catty affair."

"Catty, hairball," Sir grumbled, associating the words with the likes of a cat while sitting under Valena's chair with what little hair he had standing up on his back.

"What exactly is the Hair Ball all about?" asked Valena.

Horrible disregarded her question.

"What about your little friend? Does he want his hair done too?" mocked Horrible.

"Funny," Sir retorted quietly. "At least I don't look like a porcupine that was hit by a windstorm."

Valena sat down on the cold chair. Shway, disguised as Dr. Snipper Lopper Bottom, stepped forward. He juggled the hair tools up into the air, began to snip at her hair, and sang, "It's show time!" He yelled the words loudly. "Let me introduce myself," he bowed to Valena.

My name is Snipper Lopper Bottom,
I'll snip your hair right off.
I'll chop it from the bottom or I'll cut it from
the top,
I'll snip and snip away until your hair is all
lopped off.
I'll take care of all your problems, pigtails,
wigs, or mops.
For I'm the best hairdresser the land has ever
seen,
and there've been times when people say,
that I am rather mean.
My name is Snipper Lopper Bottom,
I'll snip your hair right off.
I'll tint it, crop it, tie it, knot it, even make it
polka-dotted.
I can cut it, straighten it, bend it, break it, and
make a bouffant do,
I can stretch it out or shrink it up or even make
it blue.
So if you're feeling your hair is bad,
just come to me and I'll make you glad.
For my name is Snipper Lopper Bottom.

"Ta da! How do you like it?" said Shway, holding up a shiny piece of metal as a mirror and showing Valena what Snipper Lopper Bottom had done to her hair. It was a mess. He had tried everything, even the jaws of life couldn't cut the dirt out of Valena's hair.

"How does it look?" Valena asked enthusiastically.

Trying to control his anger, Horrible's face went ten shades of red.

"My lovely little lady, your hair is so strong it needs to come off another way," he suggested.

"I tried everything," Shway explained, wiping the sweat from his forehead, his fingers stinging from the salt, then he packed everything up—the bent scissors, the broken hedge trimmer, and the jaws of life.

"If you come to the Hair Ball tonight," Horrible proposed, "I promise I will get the dirty hair off your head."

"Oh, thank you. You are so kind," said Valena sweetly.

"You're welcome," Shway said graciously, tipping his head. He was mesmerized by her beauty. They bid Valena and Sir a good day.

"Get our horses, Shway," Horrible said bluntly.

The two men abandoned the hair salon and road off back into the forest.

"A Hair Ball, hmmm a Hair Ball?" Valena questioned herself. "Sir, I think they were rather…Sir?" Valena looked around, Sir was nowhere to be seen. Valena put her hood back on, feeling disappointed that her first visit to a hairdresser was a flop.

Sir had become impatient waiting for Valena, he had taken it upon himself to wander into the forest to stretch his legs and get a breath of fresh air.

"Sir!" called Valena. She received no answer. There wasn't a dog in sight. "Oh, Sir, you are a royal pain in the Picket Pretoff," Valena said, discouraged.

Valena started looking about for Sir, it seemed as though the sun had moved and big dark silver clouds had moved in. The forest was damp and everything looked the same. There were random holes and small mounds of earth with fresh new pieces of grass and tree growth upon them. Valena stepped over pieces of broken cement scattered around the ground and she felt strange, as though someone was watching her, so she tried to hurry and not think of silly Aunt Posey's stories of how strange things lived in the forest. Suddenly she tripped over the end of a board that was partially sticking above the ground. On the end of the board were large letters that read 'EC.' Strange, Valena thought. She bent down and began to pull the board out of the ground. She wiggled it around then pulled as hard as she could. Out it came. A long wooden heavy sign landed right on her as she fell backwards to the ground. She flipped the board off of her and read it.

"ECAE," said Valena slowly. "What is ECAE?" She noticed a letter was partially weathered off at the end of the strange word. I wonder what it stands for, Valena thought to herself. She continued to look for Sir, he was nowhere in sight. Valena was getting cold and tired.

Having a mind of his own, Sir had run deep into the forest. Standing on a mound of earth that gave him somewhat of a view of the forest, Sir began to daydream. He imagined himself as a great knight dressed in a suit of shining armour with a big sword, fighting a fearsome opponent and saving a damsel in distress.

"On guard, take that!" he said, yelling towards his opponent.

He panted heavily as he fought his enemy fiercely, then his opponent went down. Sir stood proudly, he bowed his head with one back paw upon the chest of the bad knight, he bowed towards his damsel in distress then removed his helmet. As he did he heard his damsel calling his name.

"Sir!" Valena called desperately.

Sir suddenly realized that Valena was on the hunt for him. His instincts caused him to ignore her as he was enjoying the fresh air and had found a fresh pile of earth in which to dig a big hole.

Valena's cries were heard by Mossy, a gigantic fir tree covered with strands of moss.

"Treemendous, wake up," whispered Mossy, and swished one of her huge mossy branches over an old log beside her with his centre rotted out.

"What, what?" grumbled Treemendous, who had been in a deep sleep.

"A visitor," stated Mossy.

"Tell them to go away," said old Treemendous.

"Hello, over here. I see your little dog," Mossy called out.

Valena looked around, Mossy wasn't hard to spot. She was the grandest tree in the forest.

"Wow, you're huge, and you can talk," said Valena, "My dog can talk, too."

"More weirdoes," grumbled Treemendous.

"Be nice to the young lady, she has lost her little dog," said Mossy kindly. "I'm old Mossy, I have lived here in the forest for over four hundred and ten years," she said proudly.

"You mean you're old and mossy," piped up Treemendous.

"I'm Valena," Valena said, as she curtsied to Mossy and then to Treemendous.

"That's Treemendous you're standing beside," warned Mossy.

"Is he old too?" asked Valena.

"I'm afraid so," Mossy said sadly.

"Many years ago there was a terrible fire in this small part of the forest. Why, I remember, back in the day I had the nicest fir branches in the forest. Now they're slumped with moss and my husband, Treemendous, well…" sighed Mossy, "he was an important part of the legend but he was burnt down and destroyed."

Treemendous cleared his throat.

"I was the grandest of all the trees in this forest. Why, I even became a clock and could tell time. Back in my day everything was handmade. Many of my friends left the forest and went out into the world to become important pieces of furniture, me, I stayed behind and got burned, and here I lay."

"Oh, you seem very wise," Valena complimented him. "I bet you've even seen ghosts."

"There aren't any ghosts here, are there Treemendous?" Mossy said, hinting to him slyly.

"I thought I might have…no," joked Treemendous.

"Don't frighten the little girl," Mossy said, scolding him.

"I've lived in the forest for four hundred and ten years, never even seen one yet," Treemendous replied with a yawn.

Mossy pointed with one of her large branches towards an earth mound.

"There he is, your dog, on top of the dirt pile," Mossy informed Valena.

"Better get him before a ghost does," laughed Treemendous.

Valena turned and looked, saw her dog had dug himself a hole. It wasn't like Sir to get dirty. She walked towards him. All of a sudden Valena heard Sir yelp, then saw him fall into the earth from the top of the dirt pile where he had been digging.

"Oh, no!" yelled Valena loudly. "Treemendous, give me a branch." Valena ran back and snapped a skinny green branch off the old log, the only one he had grown in years.

"Ouch," groaned Treemendous, in pain. "You hardly know me, and at my age snapping a twig can set you back."

"You will always be Treemendous to me," Mossy consoled him lovingly.

Back to sleep went old Treemendous, even with all the commotion going on around him.

Valena ran towards the dirt pile, knelt down and yelled into the hole for Sir. She stuck the tree branch down into the hole in the earth where Sir had fallen. Mossy was still looking on.

"Pfft...ghost," she sputtered, then gave her large mossy trunk a good shake and watched Valena intensely.

As Valena held the branch down inside the hole she heard a snap, it broke.

"Sir!" she cried out desperately.

All of a sudden the loose earth around the hole collapsed, Valena fell into the opening.

Up above, old Mossy covered her big mossy face with two of her massive branches to hide.

"Ghosts!" Mossy cried, as her big trunk trembled.

Down and down Valena went, like there was no end to the fall. She felt like she was being sucked down like a vacuum, then suddenly the burst of an opening parachute sounded and her fall was broken by something soft and moist that was glowing of silver. Why, this can't be, she thought to herself. It was a giant sweet pea. She floated gently downward inside the very heart of the big flower. It enveloped her like a soft hug. Valena couldn't see much, only the strange glistening of giant petals that had a sweet aroma. She shook her head a few times, opened and closed her eyes, and thought maybe this was just a weird dream. Suddenly the big flower turned upside down, opened up, and released her out into the earthy hole with a forceful sneeze of sparkling titanium dust. She finally landed in the darkness and rubbed her bottom after landing on a hard wooden floor.

Down below the surface of the earth lay a huge musty dark cavity that Sir and Valena had fallen into.

"Sir, are you in here?" whimpered Valena. "It's dark and I can't see anything."

"Will you kindly remove your fingernails from my snout?" Sir asked politely. "And if it makes you feel any better, I can't see you either."

"Sir, we're in trouble," said Valena upset.

"Really, let's make a list, invite a few close friends, throw a soiree," Sir piped up.

"Look what you've gotten us into, Sir," said Valena, as her eyes began to adjust to the darkness. "You're filthy and covered in dirt."

"Say it isn't so," Sir said in a cheeky manner.

"How will we get back out?" Valena said, speculating. "Wooo...Maybe there's ghosts down here." Sir bolted right into her arms.

"Oh, Sir, I'm joking," Valena said, holding him in her arms like a baby then gently putting him back down beside her. She could see a faint light coming in through a beautiful but dirty piece of stained glass above her on what seemed to be a wooden wall.

Wow, this is neat. Where are we? Valena thought to herself, as her eyes began to adjust even more. As she knelt, Valena felt around then stood up. The walls of this place were rounded and made of wood. On one side was a door with an old brass doorknob, against the other wall was a small table with two small stools on either side. This place looked very old and was filled with many strange trinkets. Sir sat very still, he could see what was coming.

"Yep, here we go," he said under his breath, then he closed his eyes. He didn't want to see anymore.

"Could we have fun in here, Sir," Valena said excitedly. "This is magnificent."

At each end of this huge cavity were purple velvet coach seats.

"This is like a small house," said Valena.

"It's a Gypsy caravan," said Sir seriously.

Valena wasn't listening to him. She looked up and saw beautiful sweet peas growing on the ceiling of the caravan. There was an old torn purple lace dress hanging on a silver heart-shaped hook. Over it lay an old white dirty woollen shawl. Valena looked down.

"What's in the box?" she said, opening a large wooden box. There lay a pair of dark silver boots with flowers on them, dark silver gloves, and a long dark silver flowered dress.

"Oh, I'm going to try this lovely dress on," Valena said, wondering who all this stuff could have belonged to.

"It's not nice to pry into other peoples things, leave the clothes alone," Sir warned her.

"Come on, Sir, let loose, have some fun! How often do you get stuck in a place like this with your best friend," said Valena, looking around for more stuff.

"Oh goody, knock yourself out," said Sir jokingly, wanting to get out of this damp place. "A bubble bath, a football game, an escape hatch. Just an idea!"

"Here, Sir, you can wear this shiny blue and purple stone necklace," Valena said sweetly, removing it from an old jewellery box, putting it around his neck. "It's you," she smiled.

Sir posed like a mannequin then looked at Valena like she had gone silly on him.

Valena saw a purple star-shaped glass perfume bottle. An extremely old tarnished tea service sat on a wooden shelf. Beside it hung a turquoise velvet bag covered with old purple lace. The bag was drawn shut with what looked like strands of long silver hair. Why, this looks like my hair thought Valena, looking puzzled. Next to the bag hung a strange-looking musical instrument. It was a squeeze box. Valena took it down. Putting her hands into the straps, she tried pulling it out then pushing it in, a terrible squawking sound came out. Sir covered his ears as Valena's face took on a sour expression. She couldn't figure out how this odd instrument should be played.

"What an awful sound," she said, putting it back, then lifted the velvet bag down from its hook. Sir watched in anticipation.

"It's beautiful," said Valena, "and it's quite heavy."

"Maybe it's an old keepsake," said Sir.

He watched Valena open the bag. She pulled out a long brightly-coloured scarf with silver threads lacing through it. Suddenly a misty white aura started to twist about the room. Then the scarf broke free from Valena's hands.

"Ooh, la, la," said a voice that seemed to be coming from the scarf as it made a trail of bright colours, twisting its way in circles around the caravan.

Sir braced himself against the wall, then motioned for Valena with one of his paws, let's get out! But before they could, the smell of lavender spread through the caravan. Valena threw the bag onto the couch and froze in fear. A poof of purple smoke brought Zeezee, a human-sized white Gypsy cat to life.

The cat was overly dressed in musty Gypsy attire. Layers upon layers of colourful clothing covered her funny looking furry white body. She wore many cat bells around her neck and rings on her fingers and toes. Bracelets of silver hugged her furry arms. Sir fainted at the sight of a cat so huge, the necklace slid from his small body onto the floor. Zeezee batted her long white eyelashes, grazing her eyelids which were painted with bright sparkling pink eye shadow to compliment the purple bandana wrapped around her fuzzy head. Her crooked ears stuck out. Her lipstick was clumped and ran into her fur. On her face were stiff metallic whiskers that she didn't seem to like. She kept pushing at them with her giant paws. Her stale perfume filled the caravan and her grand entrance was frightful.

The giant feline swished the layers of her brightly coloured Gypsy skirt towards Valena's legs.

"Hi honey. Who was smart enough to let this cat out of the bag, was it you? Thanks." She laughed loudly as she twirled her furry body around while playing her brass finger symbols. Then she winked at Sir, who had somehow managed to recover from his fainting spell and was trying to blend in with the furniture.

"Phew, I've been trapped in this bag ever since that horrible man burnt down our peaceful Gypsy village," Zeezee meowed.

Sir gave the cat a look that said he thought she should have stayed in the bag.

Spinning around slowly, Zeezee introduced herself.

"I'm Zeezee, the wise Gypsy fortune telling feline."

Valena was frozen, as if in a dream. Zeezee magically fanned out four beautiful heart-shaped, solid titanium lace-backed playing cards that seemed to magically appear from behind her furry head. They glittered as she laid them face up on a table. They read love, friendship, peace and honesty.

"Give me your hand," Zeezee said to Valena as she pushed down on the girl's frail shoulders, sitting her on one of the small stools. Before Valena could say anything, Zeezee's kaleidoscope eyes were staring right into hers. Zeezee reached up inside one of her sleeves and, from a secret pocket, pulled out a crystal ball the size of a cue ball. Inside it was a glowing titanium sweet pea. Sir crept to the edge of the velvet couch to see what this human-sized cat was about to do to Valena. He curled up his lip out of instinct, in a growl. The big cat turned and looked at him out of the corner of her strange eyes and hissed as a warning to back away.

"Meow," she purred, "the great Zeezee will now tell you your fortune. In one hand I hold the crystal ball in the other I hold the hand of the one who shall rule over the lost

Gypsy village of Ecae, and bring peace back to their land."

"I'm..." Valena interrupted.

"Shhh...do not speak. I look now into the crystal ball. Ah, you are Valena, how nice to meet you."

"It's nice—" Valena spoke too soon.

"Shhh," said Zeezee again. "You must concentrate while I tell you of your future and past."

Valena stared at the cat's crazy eyes as Zeezee looked piercingly into hers.

"Not just anyone can have their fortune read by the great Zeezee," whispered the cat.

Sir thought she was a foolish feline, and a snooty cat at that.

Zeezee put the crystal ball down on the table then cupped Valena's hand in her large paws.

"'Twas your grandmother that cast a spell upon your village and its people, and you, my dearest one, were born in the forest with a transparent heart," Zeezee gently told her.

"A heart with no colour?" questioned Valena, shocked.

"Soon after you were born you were rescued

by the great King Isaac. Earlier that night his evil brother, Horrible Horribin, burnt down your ancestors' Gypsy village. You have something he needs. You are the Gypsy heiress, the only one left that holds the secret to the titanium, and the one who will create peace through a change of colour within your heart."

"But, where do I get my colours from?" asked Valena.

"You will find them when you learn about Ecae, then you will set all the people free to love in peace again," Zeezee explained.

"I don't understand," said Valena.

"Without you, the secret of your village will be gone forever."

"What secret?"

"Listen to me," Zeezee purred seriously, "the Tainted Knight wants the head of the Gypsy who has the titanium hair."

Valena looked terrified by this whole situation. Maybe this is a dream, she thought. Maybe Sir is right. I have way too big of an imagination.

Zeezee lowered her voice, she held Valena's hand tightly then rolled the crystal ball across the table. It fell down onto Valena's lap. She flinched.

"Don't move," ordered Zeezee. The titanium flower inside the ball glowed brightly. Then the flowers on the ceiling of the caravan began to glow softly.

Zeezee then took Valena's hood off, and strands of her hair and her eyebrows glowed with the brilliance of the titanium sweet pea flowers. Valena could feel her scalp tingling. She felt strong yet peaceful. As the sweet smell of flowers filled the caravan, Zeezee started a peaceful Gypsy chant, an important message for the young Gypsy maiden.

Valena, sweet Valena you will find ECAE,
it's part of our world when we're fast asleep.
Protect the heirloom locket you are soon to hold,
In a child's hand imprints in the village wall is where it goes,
then teach love and peace wherever you go.

Then, with another puff of smoke, Zeezee was gone just as strangely as she had come. Sir admitted to himself he may have misjudged her character. As he looked about the caravan he noticed a dirty little white cat sitting on the velvet bench across from him. It jumped up and ran out of the caravan. Sir took off after it at once. Valena was still in shock. As Sir clawed his way out from the dark cavity of the caravan in pursuit of the cat, a large set of hands were waiting to grab him. He was stuffed into another dark place, a mouldy rotten drawstring pouch that had been doused with a powerful black sleeping dust that Horrible had prepared in order to control him after he was kidnapped.

"Help!" winced Sir, feeling very groggy—it was too late. The last he heard was the thunderous sound of horse's hooves pounding on the dirt. "It's just not my day," he slurred, as the powerful sleeping dust took effect and he fell into a deep sleep.

Valena was still down inside the cold dark caravan. This must have been a Gypsy queen's caravan, she thought. It's been down under here for all these years and somehow I'm related to this whole cat situation and this Gypsy caravan as well. Valena stood up to put the pretty bag back on the hook. The crystal ball fell onto the floor from her lap. She checked the bag once again, no Zeezee. Valena picked up the crystal ball and put it into her cloak pocket, then she stepped up onto the stool under the hole and somehow, magically, reached the top and climbed out. Strange, she thought, that was surprisingly easy. As a matter of fact, it seemed closer to the top than the distance she had fallen. She lay on the cool ground and rubbed her eyes. Grey clouds dragged themselves across the sun that sat high in the sky and seemed so bright. Valena called Sir, but he was not to be seen. Not again, she thought, and looked around.

The big giant tree that called herself Mossy just blended in with all the rest and didn't seem to exist anymore. Treemendous just lay there as though he was part of the forest too.

Valena walked back through the trees towards Kermack who had been sleeping in the shade under a tree, waiting for her by the roadside. She called loudly for Sir once again, then climbed up on the cart and pulled her cloak over her head. She was sure that Sir would be somewhere up ahead on the road. She looked back into the flower cart, wondering if he was hiding there waiting to play a game as he sometimes did. He was not there. Tears started to fill Valena's eyes. She fought her sadness, snapped the reins and Kermack started moving. Now it was just the two of them.

"If only I wasn't so curious, it's all my fault. I've lost my birthday friend!" Valena cried. She wiped her eyes with the sleeve of her dirty cloak. Kermack looked back at her then bent his head down. As he plodded along big tears fell from his eyes like small glass beads and dropped to the ground. He knew there would come a time when he wouldn't be with her either.

Valena rambled on to herself the rest of the way through the forest, talking about Sir and how much trouble she was going to be in when she got home. Kermack lent an understanding ear to her as they neared the end of the forest.

NINE

⤸✕⤹

The Tainted Knight

Valena was late for her flower deliveries. Faithful old Kermack was languishing from the long day. They were travelling as fast as Kermack's hooves could move but Valena was sure tea time had come and gone up in Zymurgy castle. Finally they came to the clearing just beyond the forest wall. Valena could see the grandest castle in all the land off in the distance. Its high majestic towers stood tall and beautifully detailed stained glass windows depicted the art of an English garden scene. White blossoms rested themselves upon creeping ivy vines that thickly covered the grey stone walls. Cemented rock supported extended rooms that jutted out from the massive structure of the castle walls.

Valena turned off the rocky road and headed up a narrow dirt pathway. This was the only way up into the castle of Zymurgy. The path led upward through a dishevelled graveyard which went to the very top where the moat surrounded the castle walls. Kermack's hooves clicked and clopped up the pathway. Valena looked from side to side, determined not to share any more of her day with spirits. Kermack started to slow down.

"Come on, Kerm, we're almost there," Valena encouraged.

With a loud clunk, the flower cart came to a complete stop.

"Please, Kermack," Valena pleaded in vain. "Oh, no use, you are so stubborn. I'll get you a carrot and some water at the top," she offered.

Kermack wouldn't budge.

"All right then, I'll have to walk you to the top," she said, exasperated. She started to climb down, then stopped.

She heard the neighing of a horse in the distance. Down a little hill off to the side of the graveyard was a dark-haired young gentlemen astride a well groomed large black and white cob horse. He was frolicking by an apple tree, picking off the luscious red apples and juggling them high into the air and laughing. Then he noticed Valena. He turned his horse and came riding in her direction up and around the tombstones as if it was a game to him. Valena watched him in amazement. She recognized him, he was the Prince of Zymurgy, they had met before but somehow he seemed different, all grown up. Valena thought she might have a friendly conversation with him even though Rosey and Posey had told her many times just to curtsy and say hello because she was just an ordinary girl and he was the son of the great King Isaac, so she needn't bother looking or dreaming of things that she couldn't ever have. Oh, but he's so dreamy, she thought to herself. Then, turning shyly, she pretended not to see him and jumped down off her cart. Her scarf fell from her neck onto one of Kermack's large front feet and her hood slid off of her head. She tried to fix her hair as she peered out from behind Kermack's big square nose, but the young prince had already noticed her loveliness. Valena quickly pulled her hood back up. It sat crooked and covered up part of her eyes. She tilted her head back a bit and nervously brushed the dirt from her clothes with her dirty hands. The handsome prince got off his horse and commanded it to stay.

"Are you all right?" he asked politely. "I see your horse is very tired," he bent his head around the side of Kermack's nose to see her. "We've met before, have we not? I'm Benjamin Bailey, remember?" A small shiny grey key on a chain hung from his muscular neck. "And you are?" he asked, bowing.

"Ahh…Kermack," Valena quickly replied, nervously looking into his dark green eyes.

"What a beautiful but strange name you have," he said, smiling at her.

"Oh…no, that's Kermack," Valena announced, as she pointed to her horse, "and I am," she cleared her throat, "I'm Valena, the flower girl." She curtsied sweetly.

"Yes, the flower girl. You don't look like you should be a flower girl," he said, with a funny grin that showed off the big dimples in his cheeks.

"Oh, but I am," replied Valena proudly, confused by the young man's teasing.

"I see your horse is tired, may I give him an apple or some sugar perhaps?" Benjamin asked, pulling a small leather sack of sugar cubes from the breast pocket of his clean white shirt.

"May I have one too?" Valena asked politely, noticing his green velvet cape.

"Why, you don't look like you need a grain of sugar," Benjamin said sweetly.

"I haven't eaten much all day," Valena said. She couldn't understand his sense of humour at all or why anyone would ever wear such fancy clothes to ride a horse. Benjamin laughed at her. She was very unusual with her dirty little purple dress, hooded cloak, and very odd hair that stuck out from beneath her hood.

"Is this yours?" Benjamin asked as he bent down and picked up her purple scarf, handing it to her gently.

Kermack's feet started to shuffle. Valena took the scarf then quickly turned around and jumped up onto her cart.

"Thank you. Sometimes he starts without me," she smiled as she tied her scarf around her neck. Kermack started to head up towards the big wooden drawbridge doors. Valena gave a dainty wave of her delicate hand to say goodbye. Benjamin waved back. Up the hill she went.

Kermack had done well by stopping, he looked back at Valena's face, it was the colour of a red rose. Valena saw the big wooden drawbridge doors coming down. Kermack clunked across it. Valena waved to the men who let them through. Benjamin watched her from afar. He remembered her, she was just as sweet as the first time he ever saw her with Rosey and Posey when she was just a small girl. He hadn't seen her for a long time because he had been sent away to study the art of knighthood across the lands in Kullatoon—another kingdom, far from Zymurgy—and had just come home to celebrate his sixteenth birthday. He found her as mystifying as a rainbow, an odd beauty, like a wild flower. Her voice was gentle and hypnotically different than any other girls he'd ever met, it magically drew him to her.

Suddenly he turned with a jerk and planted a big kiss right on the soft flat nose of his large horse, he leaned in close to the animal's big warm hairy ears and spoke in confidence, addressing him by his name.

"Biggs, I have to look really sharp tonight, my best, in case she's there." The large beast turned his head sideways in question, snorting, "Oh Biggs, at the big Hair Ball. Do you think she likes me? Ugh...Biggs...what if she's not there?" The horse could see Benjamin Bailey had fallen in love. Getting back up onto his horse the prince went galloping back out towards a field as though he was heading for a day at the carnival.

Valena entered a big circular courtyard where a handcrafted stained glass sculpture of a knight had been made into a beautiful water fountain clock. It was magnificent. As the daylight moved timelessly through the pieces of glass the time of day was mystically cast upon the insides of the courtyard walls, and Valena could now see time was not on her side—she was late.

Queen Annette was usually waiting in the courtyard for Rosey, Posey and Valena, but today Valena could only feel embarrassment for being late.

With a look of concern upon her soft oval aged face the queen came sauntering gracefully towards Valena, holding up her black velvet gown from the dusty cobblestones of the courtyard. Her soft grey hair had lovely little yellow roses inserted into the braid that rested on the crown of her head and her blue eyes sparkled as she smiled to welcome Valena.

"Good afternoon, Valena," said the queen.

Valena got down from her cart very gingerly.

"Your Highness," said Valena, and she curtsied low, her head almost touching the cobblestones.

"I was about to put a pigeon to flight as I felt your tardiness to be a sign of trouble," said the queen.

"We're fine, I mean, I'm fine," said Valena, embarrassed. "I hope you will forgive me, but Sir and I were caught in a terrible windstorm in the forest and my hair almost blew—" Valena's eye's bulged, remembering, she'd lost her dog.

"Sir? You have a gentleman along with you?" Queen Annette interrupted.

"Yes, well not exactly. A dog, Sir, to be exact," answered Valena.

"I love dogs," said the queen. "Where might he be?" She looked into the back of the flower cart. "I don't see him! Is he small?"

Now Queen Annette had known Rosey

and Posey for most of her life, even before she had become the Queen of Zymurgy, and sixteen years ago to this very day she had taken an oath and was sworn to secrecy about Valena being abandoned in the forest and left in the care of the spinster twins by her late husband King Isaac, who had died soon after while hunting in the forest, leaving the queen to bring up their newborn son, Prince Benjamin. Her life had been a struggle but she had kept King Isaac's secret close to her heart.

Inquisitively looking into the cart, and being as open-minded as she was, the queen wondered if Valena was telling the truth.

"Is your dog shy? Maybe he's hiding under the flowers somewhere," said the queen kindly. "After all, this is your first delivery by yourself!"

"It's also my sixteenth birthday," Valena piped up. Valena tried to fix her hair as she gazed at her reflection in the clear water in the fountain basin. Then she lost her balance and almost fell in, causing the lace on her dress to catch in the opening of her cloak.

The queen gasped then composed herself.

"I do like your dress. It's very pretty," she complimented.

"Oh, thank you! Rosey and Posey gave it to me."

The queen tried to dismiss the odd behaviour of Miss Valena.

"What kind of a dog is Sir, exactly?" asked the queen.

"He is a Picket Pretoff," said Valena proudly.

"He must be a very rare breed, I don't believe I have ever seen one."

"He told me he was…ah…I mean…yes, a very good bloodline," Valena answered.

Strange little girl, thought the queen.

"Let's call Truc, he will come get the cart and collect the flowers," said the queen, summoning Truc with a clap of her hands. Then she excused herself and slowly turned around to exit through a door back into the castle. Stopping, she turned back to Valena.

"Before I go back to my tapestry I must ask you, are you attending the Hair Ball this evening?"

Valena stared at her, not knowing what to say, as she had never really known what this Hair Ball was all about.

"I thought my son Benjamin would like

some company of his own age this evening," the queen said, then smiled, turned, and disappeared gracefully back through the doorway and into the castle.

Soon an extremely tall man, sloppily dressed, his clothes smelling of fresh earth, entered the courtyard. He swayed his oversized head from side to side, overcrowded teeth that were green with rot overlapped his bottom lip and his left eye was sewn shut. He scuffed his pigeon-toed feet towards Kermack and led the horse and flower cart back through a large arched opening behind the castle walls.

Valena sat down on the ledge of the fountain, the cool mist of the water felt good on her face. Patiently waiting for Truc to bring back her flower cart she pondered her thoughts for a short while then, looking up at the large stained glass water fountain, she wondered,

Maybe I'm just a water droplet in time,
a little purple orchid that needs some sunshine.
I'm not the girl that I used to be,
I feel another girl inside of me.
I lose one friend, I find another,

life seems so hard, I need my druthers.
For who would know we'd come and go,
my hairless friend, I love you so.
Maybe we're just water droplets in time.

Valena hung her head down, thinking about Sir and how it was all her fault that he was gone. Her tears began to fall. Unexpectedly, a friendly voice broke the silence and brought Valena back into the world again.

"Hi Valena," said a short middle-aged freckly-faced red-headed woman wearing an apron over a worn out orange satin dress that covered most of her fair skin. She felt her way across the raised cobblestones of the courtyard with her short walking stick.

"Hi, Remoh," said Valena happily.

"Oh, I'm so glad you're still here, I am so slow and my eyes haven't been able to find their way for years," said Remoh.

Valena stood up and walked towards Remoh with her arms open. They gave each other a big hug.

"I love it when you come to visit," said Remoh.

"I brought you some pretty smelling

rosebud sachets, they're in the cart, they are just for you," said Valena.

"Thank you," said Remoh, as she tapped her cane rhythmically on the ground.

"They're in a special box, Truc is unloading them right now from the flower cart," Valena told her. "Remoh, you look lovely today."

"Thank you, and you smell of beautiful flowers as always," Remoh replied.

"Your corsage is with the others," Valena told her, "a beautiful royal red orchid. I grew it myself in the garden especially for you."

Remoh was ecstatic. She was going to wear this lovely flower in her hair at the Hair Ball tonight. It would carry a scent that would throw any gentleman into a fluster and might turn a simple arrangement into a marital engagement.

As they talked, Truc brought back one very well fed and refreshed horse pulling an empty flower cart.

"Thank you for the flowers, Valena," said Truc in a very loud monotone voice, then, with a sudden mechanical turn, he dragged his lethargic frame slowly back behind the castle walls.

"You're welcome, Truc," Valena called out.

Remoh asked Valena if she might give her a ride into town to her piano lessons but, most of all, Remoh was on a mission to give Valena a gift—a very special gift, for she knew it was her sixteenth birthday today— and riding to town would be a lovely way to spend part of the day. Valena told Remoh that she had never been into the town before and would love to give her a ride and see it. When they were ready to go, the drawbridge doors opened and out they went down the dirt path and out onto the roadway.

"Is it far to town?" asked Valena.

"No," replied Remoh, "when we get there I will show you everything. Well, I guess you can see it for yourself," chuckled Remoh. "Are you going to the Hair Ball tonight?" Before Valena could answer, Remoh chirped, "Happy Birthday." She was so excited to give Valena her present. Remoh thought Valena should know some of the history behind this lovely gift that she was going to receive. Oh dear, it was so long ago, she said to herself. Then she thought deeply and recalled that the year after her brother, King Isaac, had died, Queen Annette wanted to make sure that if something happened to her, that Remoh knew all about Valena, the spinsters, and the magical stained glass Gypsy locket and titanium chain. The queen had asked her to keep the story confidential and gave Remoh the authority to deliver the heirloom in any case. Prince Benjamin had just been informed of the secret, for it was his sixteenth birthday two months ago, and he'd just come home from Kullatoon. Only just receiving the gift of the titanium key that morning, he'd taken the vow of secrecy to never tell anyone about the magical heirloom.

In-between laughter and happy conversation Remoh had thought this through enough, she reached into the pocket of her apron and pulled out a pretty grey velvet bag with something inside it. She held it carefully and spoke softly.

"My brother, King Isaac, left this gift to be given to you," she said sweetly. "After he died the queen opened a letter that was left with it and read it to me," Remoh told Valena, then started to tell her as much as she could remember of her brother's words.

"I have heard the great Gypsy tales but never did I think I would have possessed the most powerful possession of theirs. The Knight of Wishhearts stained glass heirloom locket and titanium chain. For it is said to hold the power to create peace and love and supply enough titanium to make a warrior the most powerful and richest man in all the land, but it can only be worn by a real authentic Gypsy princess on her sixteenth birthday or its powers are useless. My dear wife and family, I trust in you to keep this secret. Inside this locket is a spot in the shape of a heart, but nothing lays in its place. When I found it, it seemed as though a piece was missing. Take the key from its spot and give it to Benjamin on his sixteenth birthday, tell him to always wear the key on a chain around his neck and only take it off when the time is right. He will receive instructions when that time comes. The Gypsies say it magically unlocks a secret compartment on the caravan belonging to the great Gypsy queen. That compartment is where the real Gypsy magic begins. This gift must be given to Valena on her sixteenth birthday." Remoh paused, "And…that's it."

She smiled. She didn't want to tell Valena about the part, where, if she'd died before her sixteenth birthday they were to hide the heirloom forever, or the part about it being found sitting under a mound of warm metallic ashes on a bench in the Gypsy village after a big fire. She didn't want to ruin Valena's birthday with gory details.

Anyway, thought Remoh, there was nothing to worry about because Valena would now have the heirloom locket and young Prince Benjamin of Zymurgy had received the key which had been hidden up inside the bottom of a large candle for all these years, and the queen knew that the power of the Gypsy heirloom and its key would work together magically.

Valena listened to Remoh's story and thought back to Zeezee telling her that the secret lay within the hand imprints in the wall. It all started to fit together and Valena realized now she had come from somewhere else, and she was going to find out where even if it killed her. Remoh handed Valena the grey velvet bag. As Valena slowed Kermack down, she reached inside the bag and took out the ancient titanium necklace with its stained glass locket, the heirloom of Ecae. Valena looked at it intensely, not telling Remoh about her earlier encounter with the strange large cat.

"It's just beautiful," said Valena. "Thank you, Remoh."

Valena opened up the locket. Inside was a hollow shape for a heart and, beside it, another hollow spot for a key. She thought it nice that the king had shared the key part of her gift with his son. Valena closed the locket, put it back in the bag, then carefully put it deep inside her cloak pocket so Rosey and Posey wouldn't see it and wonder where she'd been.

"Remoh, you are very special to me, I hope you will always know that," Valena said with tears in her soft grey eyes.

"Thank you Valena, you are very special to me too," Remoh smiled shyly and put her folded fist upon her closed lips. "I'm going to the Hair Ball tonight, you should come too. I'm going dressed up as a damsel in distress and wearing a beautiful mask."

"What kind of a mask?" Valena questioned, remembering her Quimmy mask.

"I have an orange and gold feathered hummingbird mask, the queen told me it looks lovely on me," said Remoh, "and if you come to the Hair Ball I will give you a pretty one to wear, besides, I have another one that's just as suitable for the occasion, what do you think?"

"I think you will make a wonderful damsel in distress and I hope you find a brave knight to save you," said Valena, smiling.

"Are you happy right now, Valena?" Remoh asked.

"Yes," answered Valena.

"I knew it," giggled Remoh, the freckles on her nose wrinkled up as she laughed.

As they headed towards town, Valena admitted to Remoh that Rosey and Posey had given her a small dog for her birthday and he went missing in the woods. Valena saw Remoh's eyes growing wider.

"What if the Gypsy ghosts get him?" Remoh said, moving her head about with a worried look on her face.

"There's no such thing as ghosts," said Valena.

"That's not what my brother Isaac said,"

Remoh whispered. "BOO!" yelled Remoh loudly.

"Ahh!" Valena screamed, flinching in her seat. She felt somehow she deserved that and could feel Sir's presence. "Remoh, don't believe all those silly stories," said Valena.

"I'm not afraid of ghosts. Besides, I can't see them anyway," Remoh said in a matter of fact manner.

"Remoh, no one can see them—they're invisible."

"Well, if I can't see them, then they're not real," Remoh said, ending the conversation quickly. "You're smart, Valena."

"I'm not that smart," said Valena. "I've lost my balding Picket Pretoff somewhere in the big forest." She lowered her eyes and blinked quickly to hide her tears.

"Your what?" Remoh said.

"Never mind," Valena sighed.

Valena and Remoh were close to the town.

"Wait until you see the flowers around the entrance to the town, they are so lovely," said Remoh. "Inside there are dress shops and a hat store, a hair dresser and a big chocolate shop. It's the most wonderful place to go and, well, I can hardly see…but…I've always loved the piano, so I take music lessons from…Mr. Friendle. He is…a wonderful patient teacher," she added blushing.

It was now getting late and Valena needed to hurry so she gave Kermack a snap of the reins, he picked up the pace then slowed down again as usual. Finally they came to a sharp turn in the roadway which led them down into the town. Remoh was ecstatic about having the privilege of showing Valena the town for her first time, she had fond memories of her visits there with her mother, Queen Catherine of Zymurgy, before she passed away.

"After my brother King Isaac passed away, my oldest brother, Erick Horribin, who inherited the Town of Petalville by the order of an old will, had concerned townspeople gossiping. He was going to make a few small changes to the little town and told them it was going to be more exciting than before," Remoh said informatively.

"That was very kind of him," said Valena.

"Yes, and once a year, every fall, the people of the town come together to have a wonderful party called the Hair Ball," said Remoh. "That's when I come too!" she added.

"What is the Hair Ball exactly?" Valena asked.

"It's so much fun," Remoh said as she smiled. "The Hair Ball is a costume party for everyone and was made mandatory by the mayor of this town. Any girl who had reached the age of sixteen was automatically entered into the contest. This made them feel proud to be able to get up on a big stage and have a hairdresser cut their hair, then the best cut would win first prize and receive a real wig made of beautiful soft human hair."

"Well…I'm sixteen," Valena said excitedly, as she felt her hair and thought it would be a wonderful idea if she could attend as she really needed someone to do something about her terrible hair. "Do they cut off all your hair?" Valena asked.

"No, but a long time ago it was said that if you cut off the hair of a real Gypsy princess you would have many years of happiness and be the strongest and most powerful man in the land," Remoh preached.

"Remoh, my hair is weird," commented Valena. "Rosey and Posey told me to hide it or people will think I'm strange."

"One day Queen Annette found a piece of your hair in the courtyard on the cobblestones. She picked it up and commented that it was the strongest piece of silver hair she had ever seen. It was like the metal that held together the suit of a knight in shining armour," said Remoh, with a dreamy look in her eyes.

"Oh, Remoh, you are so kind," smiled Valena. "Do you think they can fix my hair at the Hair Ball?"

"Yes, come, you may even win! Then you could have a really nice wig and not have to worry about having to hide your hair any-more."

"I don't think Rosey and Posey will let me go," Valena said with a sad look.

"Don't worry, I'm sure we can think of something," said Remoh reassuringly. "We should almost be there."

In the distance Valena could see a big shiny metal structure that projected itself high in front of the entrance into the town.

"Mr. Friendle is taking me to the Hair

Ball tonight," Remoh said as she patted her heart gently, a little out of breath.

"I can't imagine going to such a party as this," exclaimed Valena as she looked towards the town of Petalville.

"Are we here yet?" Remoh asked excitedly.

As they were getting closer Valena could see that the sign in front of the town had been changed. It now read: Town of Metalville. Encircling the town were high rusted metal walls, there were no flowers anywhere.

In front of the town was a gigantic knight in ancient armour. The knight was sitting on the ground with his body split down the centre, one large metal glove held a morning star flail and the other a huge rusted sword with its sharp end partially propped up against the wall.

"Valena?" Remoh said apprehensively.

"Yes," answered Valena quickly.

"What's wrong?" Remoh asked, she could feel Valena's voice was uneasy.

"Nothing…" answered Valena, overwhelmed.

As they rode up in front of the large structure and Valena saw the monstrous knight, she began to feel afraid. From its helmet were thick burnt crawling vines that covered the gigantic parts of this ancient armour. Wilted flowers hung from the opening of its crooked mouthpiece, green moss grew from its oxidized joints, and light reflected off what little metal was left to shine from the rusted chest of the metal monster. Wide pipe-like legs lay on the ground, spread apart, with hinged joints that joined them to the large metal boots, all the way down to the toes which were pointed outward as though the monster had fallen asleep. Valena had stopped Kermack in front of it, she looked up and stared at the huge object.

"Magnificent isn't it?" Remoh said. "I can just imagine everything is all ready for the Hair Ball tonight. Let's go in and I'll show you around."

"We...should really get you to your piano lessons," stated Valena, wanting to leave as soon as possible.

"Look high up into the tower," said Remoh, "that's a real authentic Gypsy man. He doesn't talk but if you wave to him he will let us in. He is known here in this town as the Gatemaster. He opens and closes the big gated chest of the knight into the town."

Valena waved at the Gatemaster then the sound of huge clanking rusted metal chains began to rub against the metal doors and the centre of the knight's chest started to move slowly apart. As they waited to enter, Remoh told Valena the strange story of the Gatemaster.

"The people in the town are not allowed to talk to the Gatemaster because he is a bad man. My brother Horrible found him one day in his partially burnt caravan all alone deep in the forest. He had burnt down his own village. Horrible rescued him, brought him here, gave him a job, and let him keep his burnt caravan to live in. He is chained inside the tower so he won't cause any trouble for the people of this town. They are afraid of him because he never talks and is dangerous."

Valena looked up at the seemingly gruff looking man. She put her hands over her ears as the rusted knight's chest parted, the noise raked her eardrums. As rust floated around them, the smell of metal filled the cool afternoon air. Kermack pulled them through the massive structure. As they passed through to the other side, Garth recognized the 'E' that was branded on the rear of the old horse; the young girl resembled the Gypsy queens and she had the silver blue eyes of a wolf like him. She was wearing the purple scarf made by the Gypsies. Garth knew now that the story Horrible had been talking about earlier was true and he became overwhelmed with emotion at seeing this lovely Gypsy girl.

"Besides the racket of that rusty old gate, what do you think?" asked Remoh.

"I think you are very late for your music lessons," Valena said nervously. Perhaps Remoh had never known about how the town had changed and somehow no one had ever told her.

Valena rode through the main part of the town, where weeds had overridden the narrow cracked, cobblestone street. Young boys were dressed in knights armour, they were sitting on metal ponies that were being pushed about in the streets, joisting each other. Loud sounds of clanging metal swords filled the air as the thudding of small, sharp, rusty metal flails were being flung about, striking each other. Shrill cries came from the mouths of smaller children who were fighting on the ground.

Young girls held swords in their hands and made angry faces towards each other. They wore metal veils on their heads and fine chain-linked metal dresses hung from their delicate shoulders from thick rusted chains. Their small feet were bound and imprisoned by dented metal boxes that were joined together at the ankles with heavy chains, keeping them from running freely. Valena watched sadly as all this took place.

Valena's head started to get hot as small pieces of her hair glowed. She felt something strange happening to her. Growing out of her temples were warm titanium sweet pea flowers that glowed on her head. Slowly she took one hand off the reins and slid it inside the hood of her cloak to feel the weird growth, then her vision started turning like a kaleidoscope and she felt dizzy for a moment. The ghosts of small children appeared, trying to offer sweet pea flowers to the children that were fighting, but they didn't seem to know they were even there. Then the ghost-like children gently disappeared, as did the warmth of her hair and the flowers upon her head. Valena felt frightened but kept this to herself while watching the children playing the worst games she had ever seen.

"Valena, isn't this great? The children are screaming and having so much fun, everyone here must be preparing for this special evening," said Remoh. "Can you see all the nice stores, Valena? One day you should get Rosey and Posey to bring you here for afternoon tea. This must be so exciting for you," Remoh said as she smiled.

"Yes..." Valena said, hesitating, she really didn't know quite what to think or say.

As Kermack led them through town Valena looked around and noticed there were no flower shops, no hat shops, no dress shops, and there certainly wasn't any chocolate shop. There were only metal buildings with no windows, just doors that had big heavy padlocks hanging from them. Heavy rusted chains held down rooftops that were made of level sheets of dull metal, upon them sat large square incinerators with ashes that swirled about in the wind as warm cinders still smouldered inside them. Everything was dingy and cold looking.

The people of the town wandered the streets and were unhappy. Even their dogs were a sad sight to see. The cobblestones were packed with weeds that grew high up through the stones, trying to breathe. As Valena and Remoh got deeper into the town the people stared at them and went into their homes and locked the doors. They seemed disturbed by their presence. Kermack's hooves cracked sharply on the rocks. Valena had an awful time finding the music shop. Hanging metal signs were worn and hard to read, so rusted she couldn't see the names. Valena felt sick, she couldn't speak—someone had told poor Remoh a lie about this place. Finally Valena caught sight of a rusty old sign that was hanging crookedly from its chain. The rusted letters read: Friendle's Music Shop. Valena pulled in front of his store and stopped.

"We're here aren't we," said Remoh with a smile. "Oh, thank you Valena. I hope you enjoyed seeing the town. Please come to the Hair Ball tonight. I am so—" Remoh's voice was muffled by the loud sound of a big black stallion's hooves bolting through the streets straight towards them.

Some of the children who had still been fighting quickly moved out of the way of this gigantic horse. They stood at attention on the side of the street admiring the person who rode in on this large animal. Valena looked back, the large horse was coming right up behind them. Remoh froze, she could now feel the tension in the air.

The big horse's hooves slowed down, clipped the cobblestones, and dug up the weeds from the ground. Cracked cobblestones were driven farther down into the earth by this heavy animal. Horrible Horribin sat high upon his mean horse, acting as though he were the king himself. He rode right up beside the sweet Gypsy girl and Remoh, bringing his horse to a halt.

Kermack lurched the flower cart backward warning him not to come any closer. Everyone had gone into their homes now, the streets were empty. Silence hovered over the little town like a dark cloud. Nothing moved except the chain on the sign hanging over Mr. Friendle's music shop. It creaked as a late afternoon breeze moved it slightly back and forth, then it stopped.

"Well, we must be here," said Remoh, not understanding the silence.

Just then Oscar Friendle came quickly out of his music shop. He was the finest pianist in the land and well known for his big shiny metal grand piano, it was his prize possession, it took him five long years to design and make the piano himself. Other than his piano, Mr. Friendle adored his two faithful friends, Hubert and Humphrey, his big hairy friendly pigs. They went everywhere together, and often took Mr. Friendle, in his homemade barrel pig cart, across the countryside to entertain for the royal families. This is where, as a young man, he first laid eyes on the sweet young Princess Remoh. In his eyes she was still as lovely as the Sonatina that he had played for her and her family many years ago. He always took her safely home right after her lessons and left a kiss upon her hand.

As Mr. Friendle approached the cart he stopped and raised his head to look up at Horrible, who was glaring at him with his evil eyes. Mr. Friendle carefully moved around the flower cart and helped Remoh down.

"Thank you again, Valena," said Remoh. As Mr. Friendle escorted her into his music shop he told her he would only be a minute, then gave her a gentle shove through the open door for she knew her way to the big metal piano. Then he shut the door and stood outside, pasted into the doorframe. He felt something awful was going to happen because he'd never seen this young girl in the town before and Horrible looked deeply disturbed by her.

Valena sat in her cart, she didn't move. She now knew that there was something bad about this town and the man on the big black stallion. As Mr. Friendle stood in the doorframe Valena could see his small frame shaking. He kept fussing nervously with his messy light blonde hair, pushing it back with his stubby sweaty hands. Upon his small ski jump nose sat a wire-rimmed pair of glasses. He twitched and blinked his eyes as though the light of day was too bright for them, while trying to focus on Horrible Horribin's large horse. Horrible sneered as his horse walked over and nibbled on the shoulder of poor Mr. Friendle's green tweed suit. His forehead became soaked with perspiration as his body temperature rose like a thermometer, for he had a terrible fear of horses. Valena noticed a sign that was posted outside the music shop.

The One and Only Metal Piano in the World
will be
played this evening at the
Hair Ball,
by the talented pianist
Mr. Friendle himself.

Just below that sign was a poster that read:

THE
ANNUAL HAIR BALL
Anyone sixteen and over, apply for the competition.
First prize will be a real soft human hair wig.

The infamous Horrible had been searching for years for the head of hair that grew only on a certain girl. He knew that this girl held the secret to the Gypsy heirloom for she did not have a head of silver, nor even of gold, but a head of hair that held titanium strands. Even Valena didn't fully know the powers that she possessed.

"Valena," said Horrible, greeting her in a grandiose manner. "It's a pleasure to see you again."

Valena adjusted the purple bow around her neck, making sure it was tightly tied. She peered out from beneath her cloak as though Horrible was going to spit on her. This time she was wise to him and remembered what Rosey and Posey had said about her hair.

"I see my friend Mr. Friendle has made you welcome in my little town," Horrible said slyly.

"Yes, he has," Valena said, "but I must be going now. I have to—" The wicked man brought her sentence to a stop with a terrible lie.

"Why, my dear Friendle was just telling me earlier today that he was thinking of asking you to the Hair Ball." He was hoping the innocent young Gypsy girl wouldn't catch on.

"But…I have a student right now," said Mr. Friendle.

"Friendle, I mean Mr. Friendle, do you like your job?" provoked Horrible.

"Yes . . ." replied dear Mr. Friendle.

"Then, perhaps after you ask Miss Valena to the Hair Ball, you might find you still have it."

Mr. Friendle felt a lump in his throat. He could hardly swallow as he had already extended an invitation to Remoh. Valena noticed Mr. Friendle's face. It dropped, as his heart fell down into his stomach.

"Why, uhh...Mr. Friendle and I barely know each other," said Valena nervously, trying to detour the madman. "And Rosey and Posey, well...they need me to care for the house while they're out this evening enjoying the Hair Ball."

Mr. Friendle felt relieved as Valena tried to outfox Horrible, but he always had a dastardly plan up his sleeve and was now about to pull another one right out of a dusty black bag that hung from the side of his horse.

"Look here, what's in the bag," said Horrible in a high voice, looking straight at Valena. He took the bag from his horse and held it up in the air over the back of the empty cart. Dangling from his bony finger, the bag swung slowly back and forth. Horrible then opened the bag, reached in, and grabbed a groggy little dog by its collar and yanked it out.

"Sir," Valena said, shocked.

"Oh, a little groggy doggy," grimaced

Horrible. Sir was choking as Horrible held him tightly an inch away from his face. Sir struggled and tried to bite the end of Horrible's large, crooked nose.

"Were you lost, and I found you?" Horrible said as he moved Sir about like a puppet on a string.

"My dog! You found my birthday present!" Valena cried, her hood slid back slightly as she went to take Sir from Horrible's tight grip.

"Not yet, birthday girl," Horrible said gruffly, as he held Sir in his grip. "With your beautiful hair and lovely disposition you should be able to win first prize at the Hair Ball tonight! Me, I could use a new pet, take him home, whip your little precious into shape...what do you say? Is that a...YES!" he threatened.

"No! I mean, Mr. Mayor, King, Sir..." Valena pleaded. Her heart fell into the pit of her stomach. She felt frightened and knew that if she didn't do what this wicked man said she wouldn't get Sir back.

"Well, I guess I could go...if you give back my dog," Valena said in desperation.

"It's a deal and I love deals," said Horrible

with a sick smile. He then turned slowly towards Mr. Friendle who hadn't moved a muscle. "Mr. Friendle will pick you up this evening at seven o'clock sharp, won't you Friendle. Now, go back to your student."

Mr. Friendle bid Valena a good afternoon, he felt much smaller than he physically appeared. He hung his head in shame for he knew he was part of a terrible plan, then he quickly went back into his music shop and closed the door tightly. Horrible dropped Sir into the back of Valena's empty cart where he landed with a thud then quickly jumped back up onto his feet.

Then Horrible took off on his big horse and disappeared through the open chest of the knight.

"How dare that man treat me in such a gruff manner," Sir complained, sticking his snout high into the air while shaking the remainder of the black sparkly dust off his body.

"Oh, I see you're okay," said Valena.

"Nothing fazes my breed, now let's get out of here," Sir said, looking back over his shoulder.

The gates through the knight were still

open. Valena turned her horse and cart around and went galloping out through the doors. Kermack was very glad to be going home, his feet were sore and some weeds were stuck in them, not to mention fluff from some dandelions was stuck up his nostrils. He gave a big sneeze which sent his nerves into a frenzy. After exiting the town, Valena looked back and saw the old Gypsy man waving goodbye to them.

He doesn't look like a bad man, thought Valena.

Sir was so happy to see Valena again that he sat up proudly beside her all the way back home.

"Sir, I love you," said Valena. Sir jumped onto Valena's lap. "Giddy up Kermack," yelled Valena.

"Yes, we haven't got all night," Sir commented.

The three of them headed homeward, racing against sundown. They finally reached the pathway leading back up into the gardens around Flower Petal Cottage.

"Now, I can't talk," said Sir to himself. This was going to be a difficult thing for this little rascal of a dog.

TEN

❧✗❧

The Hair Ball

Kermack was slower than ever. He plodded past the gardens and over to the cottage, the three had returned home safely. Valena stopped Kermack and tied him to the big apple tree beside the barn. As she had gotten down from her cart, she'd spotted some red apples laying on the ground. She picked up a few and tried to juggle them.

"He's not the only one that can juggle apples," Valena frowned as they instantly fumbled to the ground. "How did he do that?" she mumbled, thinking of the kind handsome prince that had helped her earlier today. Valena remembered the queen had mentioned that he would be attending the Hair Ball tonight. So all I have to do is recognize him in his costume, Valena thought. I wonder what he'll wear? Then Valena began to daydream, she danced around the apple tree and sang to it as if it were the prince himself, she lost all track of time.

The royal gentleman may ask me to dance, as a
gallant prince would do,
he'll bow, I'll curtsy, we'll dance away, in our
favourite party shoes.
We'll wish together in a forest of dreams,
kiss the rays of a moonbeam that autumn
brings.
Then he'll gaze into my eyes.
The world will spin, wedding bells will ring,
it won't be a dream, but a real life thing.
And in love we'll marry, and become king and
queen.

Sir had jumped down off the flower cart and was watching Valena.

"She's dancing with an apple tree," he mumbled to himself. "Valena. Valeeeenaaaa... VALENA!" Sir called, putting himself at risk.

"What?... What?... Oh, yes, yes, yes... I have to hurry," Valena, now humming, started brushing off any dirt that was left on her clothes from earlier in the day and straightened her hood. Suddenly she remembered her beautiful feathered mask was down under a board in the back of her cart. Before taking it out she looked around to make sure no one was watching her then reached in and pulled out the mask and admired it. She quickly hid it inside one of her wide cloak sleeves then checked to make sure the locket necklace was still safe, deep down inside her pocket.

Why, I could wear this tonight, she thought to herself.

"Come on, Sir," called Valena, not noticing he had already jumped off the cart. Together they scurried in through the cottage door.

"I'm terribly sorry I'm late," said Valena rather nervously.

Posey asked Valena to go back and close the door behind her, the early evening fall air was beginning to invite itself in. A warm fire burned in the cast iron stove, keeping the cottage warm. Sir headed straight for his water bowl to quench his thirst. Beside it sat another bowl filled to the brim with warm mashed butter potatoes. They truly know how to treat a Picket Pretoff in this palace, he thought. Having eaten like a little pig, he gave a cumbersome burp and dragged his full belly over to the big oval rug that lay in front of the warm stove.

Valena took her usual seat at the table as Posey was hurrying about trying to get supper over with.

"My dear, you are quite late. Where on earth have you been?" she questioned Valena, who had a look of concern on her face. And old eagle eyes, Aunt Rosey, was sitting across from Valena and thumping her skinny finger tips loudly upon the table in a domino pattern while glaring at Valena, who squirmed uncomfortably in her chair.

"Valena, take off your cloak, you're going to have dinner now," said Rosey sternly.

"I'm rather chilled," Valena said, pretending to be cold. She didn't want to remove her cloak for fear the mask she was planning to wear to the Hair Ball this evening would slip out and be seen.

"I suppose Kermack is tired out and won't make it to town for the most exciting event of the year," said Rosey, annoyed.

Posey's dinner smelled heavenly throughout

the cottage. She had made her special Hidden Carrot Soup. Posey told Valena that she needed to eat lots of soup until her eye-sight was so good that she could find the carrots. Of course Valena never could find any carrots at all. Nevertheless, the soup was delicious.

"How was your first day?" Rosey asked.

As Valena swallowed hard, she felt a big lump in her throat. Sir watched her, waiting for the truth to be brought forth. And what a tangled truth she told.

"Well, the weather was absolutely horrible," exclaimed Valena.

"Oh, dear," said Posey, very concerned.

"You don't say," Rosey added smartly.

"Yes, and Sir got kidnapped and then...Oh! I met the most handsome young man," Valena explained with a dreamy look on her face. "Oh, yes, and then I gave Remoh a ride into town."

"Town?" Rosey yelled in a high shrill voice.

"Yes," Valena said breathlessly.

"Did you take off your hood?" asked Posey.

"No, never, not once," Valena lied, looking down at Sir who was afraid of what was coming next.

"Well, thank your lucky clovers for that," Rosey said, relieved.

Valena now knew something was up with these two old spinsters and how they had never told her where she'd really come from. She was determined to find out what the big secret was they had kept from her all these years. Rosey didn't eat her soup, waltzed past Valena in a huff, and went upstairs to get ready for the Hair Ball.

"Aunt Posey, could I come with you to the Hair Ball tonight?" Valena asked politely.

"My goodness, you are not old enough," commented Posey.

"But I am. The poster in town said anyone sixteen years or older can attend," explained Valena.

From the top of the stairwell and out of the mouth of an eavesdropping Aunt Rosey came a threat, as clear as could be.

"You are never to go to town again. Do you hear me?"

Valena knew better then to challenge Rosey's firecracker personality.

"Eat up the rest of your soup dear, and when you are done, tidy up and lock the door after we leave. We won't be late," instructed Posey.

"But I am old enough," Valena whined. "Please, Aunt Posey."

"No, no, no, no," sang Posey, to alleviate the stress.

Valena hung her head down. Sir lay still, hoping that Valena wasn't going to engage in anymore extra unusual activities for the rest of his life.

"I will leave you some milk and sweet cakes for later. You and Sir enjoy the warm fire. We will be home early," promised Posey, cupping Valena's soft face with reassurance, then she went upstairs to get ready

"Oh, I hate it when she's so nice to me," Valena said, frowning.

Sir hadn't moved his lazy balding Picket Pretoff body one inch from where he had laid himself down earlier. As he kept his eye on Valena he could see a silent storm welling up inside of her and hoped it would soon pass.

The twin spinsters soon came down from upstairs. Rosey was dressed all in black. A lace curtain made into a long dress draped her skinny body, a homemade hat with crumpled flowers sat high upon her head and was tied under her chin with a black silk scarf. Her black eye shadow made her eyes look like two miniature glossy marbles and her lipstick of fire engine red was hideously applied to her paper thin lips. She looked as though she was going to a funeral.

Posey was wearing a dress made of worn cotton dish cloths that were sewn together to make a long gown that hung oddly to the floor. It made her plump body look like a lumpy basket of bread rolls. Around her thick waist was a piece of brightly coloured yellow ribbon, pulled tight in an attempt to create a thinner waistline. Upon her head sat a funny kind of hat covered with coloured buttons of every sort. It was tied with a worn ribbon that fit into the folds under her chin. Posey carried a dainty hanky in her hand and waved it about. She was doused in talcum powder and it flew everywhere, making Rosey choke. Sir thought they looked like they had lost their minds. He watched as they hurried about, putting on their matching woollen shawls. Sir closed his eyes and thought, I will not laugh, I will not laugh. He struggled to control himself, almost bursting with laughter.

"It's time to go, Rosebud," said Posey, staring at her sister strangely.

"Oh, yes," Rosey replied, waving her hands in front of her face and trying not to sneeze.

"Lovely hair styles, you both look very elegant," said Valena sweetly.

They pinned each other's purple orchids on then Posey grabbed Rosey's hand and danced towards the door. Rosey yanked her hand back.

"Let's go," said Rosey, looking back at Valena with sombre concern.

Out the door they went, saying goodbye to Valena.

"Remember, lock the door and stay inside, we'll be home early," called Posey.

"Yes, goodbye, have a lovely time!" Valena said, quickly closing the heavy door behind them.

The two women climbed up onto the flower cart. Kermack looked back at them as they pulled on the reins. Oh dear, a heavier load than this morning, he thought to himself, and if he had any life left in him at all, this would surely be the end of it.

Valena watched out the window and then, when her two aunts were out of sight, she ran upstairs to get ready for the Hair Ball as Mr. Friendle would be picking her up at precisely seven o'clock.

Valena sat upon the soft red blanket that covered the stool in front of her vanity table. She reached into her cloak pocket and pulled out the grey bag, then took out the beautiful necklace and admired the stained glass locket.

This was surely the most lovely piece of jewellery she had ever seen. Valena remembered what Zeezee had said, that the locket necklace needed to be protected and it belonged in a child's hand imprints in some village wall. She tried to open it but it seemed stuck. Strange, she thought, as she put it around her neck then slipped it under the collar of her dress. Then Valena gently reached up into her cloak sleeve and pulled out the beautiful Quimmy mask. She studied the pieces of her hair that were sewn in-between the feathers. They glimmered. Valena looked into her vanity mirror and put the mask on her face. Magically, shiny dark silver sweet peas appeared upon her temples like the ones she had seen on the strange dress down inside the hidden caravan. Valena was amazed. She quickly removed the mask and the flowers disappeared. When she put it on again, the flowers reappeared once more. Quickly she removed it again, feeling frightened of this strange thing that was happening to her. She gently put it back inside her sleeve and concentrated on getting ready, for Mr. Friendle would soon be here.

Valena did not notice Sir, but he had been watching her intensely from the doorway.

"Going somewhere, Miss Valena?" he inquired.

"Yes, I...I mean, we're going somewhere. We're going to the Hair Ball together," answered Valena with a big smile.

"Really," said Sir, trying his best to get out of this one. "Well then, I was thinking of going as a fearsome knight in shining armour with a huge sharp sword. I will be the most feared knight at the Hair Ball and you will be my princess," boasted Sir grandly.

"Sir!" cried Valena loudly. "You are just a

little dog. Surely you don't have a mean bone in your hairless body. Fighting is bad, Sir. You can't just go around with a big sword, killing people."

"Yes, I suppose you're right. I won't be able to go then," replied Sir, as he hung his head, put his tail between his legs, and crept slowly towards the door trying to exit.

"Nonsense, I wouldn't leave you here all alone for one minute, Sir. You may get lonely," Valena said. "Besides, the Hair Ball might be fun." As Sir turned around he sat, defeated, and rolled his eyes.

"Hair Ball is in relation to the word, CAT," Sir responded, spelling the word letter by letter for Valena with an offended look on his face.

"Oh, please come with me," begged Valena.

She ran over and picked Sir up and hugged him, then spun around the room as though they were dancing. Before he could save himself from her wild imagination, she kissed him right on the end of his nose. Yuck, human breath, he thought to himself.

Valena went over to her dresser, pulled out a drawer, and dug out one of Rosey's old holey woollen knitted socks and slipped Sir right down inside it, pulling his head and legs out through the holes. Sir looked sternly at Valena.

"As well as forgetting to let anyone know that you are going to the party, have you forgotten that I am from a long line of Picket Pretoff blood and shall not be any part of this silly costume ordeal," said Sir in a high and mighty tone.

"Please, it's all in good fun, Sir," Valena said, trying to be very serious.

"Oh, yes, I'm sure 'tis," he said.

Sir started to feel rather warm inside the itchy sock and felt quite emasculated.

"And to think, we have only been together for a short time," he commented.

Seven o'clock came quickly. Valena had only one fancy dress in her wardrobe and she was wearing it, so she supposed it would be fine. She then brushed her hair, tucked it far back under her hood, and went downstairs with Sir to wait for Mr. Friendle.

As Valena waited she heard a strange sound, like tin cans clanging together, then another sound, like pigs snorting outside the cottage. It seemed to be getting closer.

Valena peeked out a small window and could see Mr. Friendle riding in a carriage constructed from two half barrels being pulled by two huge hairy brown pigs. It stopped outside the cottage, then a strange noise rattled like a chain on the outside of the cottage door. Mr. Friendle kept clanging and rattling until Valena answered.

"Surprise, guess who?" Mr. Friendle called, with an echo coming from inside a rusted knight's helmet. Mr. Friendle was dressed in a full suit of armour that was so rusty, flakes of rust fell to the ground around him every time he moved.

"Mr. Friendle, you look very rustic tonight," said Valena as she held Sir in her arms. Sir rolled his eyes at the sight of the rusty old piece of junk that Friendle was cooped up in, not to mention his tingling nostrils from the smell of rust floating about.

"How did you know it was me?" Mr. Friendle asked, disappointed.

"Well, it wasn't easy," replied Valena, trying to be kind.

Mr. Friendle stared at Sir in Valena's arms.

"I know what your little doggy is dressed up as in his fuzzy costume. Why, he's a cat."

Sir growled and bared his teeth towards the man dressed in rusted armour.

"Be nice to Mr. Friendle or he won't take us to the Hair Ball, Sir," said Valena.

"That would be a shame," Sir mumbled under his breath.

"Well, let's get going," said Valena, looking embarrassed at Sir's bad behaviour.

Valena closed the cottage door as she left. Mr. Friendle, being the gentleman he was, helped Valena and Sir into one side of the barrelled carriage then climbed in the other side and with a stick tapped his big friendly pigs, Hubert and Humphrey, and off they went with the coloured bows on their tails bouncing.

As they left Flower Petal Cottage the sun had fully set. The big pigs stubby legs ran fast by the pond where Julia and Henry were floating asleep, then through the cold darkness of the ancient hollow tree stump. Bald Sir pulled his head inside his sock. They all huddled together through the spooky cold forest. Finally they passed the beautiful illuminated castle of Zymurgy with its ancient scary gravestones casting shadows up the hillside.

The pigs panted and snorted as they ran along through a damp fog that was settling in. Soon they approached the town of Metalville.

"We're here," Valena said, in an out of breath fashion.

"I dropped my...my...let's, go back?" blurted Mr. Friendle.

"Go back!" cried Valena. "Are you kidding! I've been dying to come here tonight."

Mr. Friendle was a nervous wreck, fidgeting with his pig's reins. He breathed heavily inside the rusted knight's helmet, knowing he had never hurt a soul in his life.

"I was thinking maybe you could go in, take a quick look around, say you've seen it all, and between you and me we will never tell anyone you escaped! I...I mean, left to go home. Then you won't get in any trouble with your aunts, you know?"

"Oh, you're so kind. You came all the way to fetch me, I wouldn't dream of making you take me all the way back. And besides, Sir wants to go, too! Right, Sir?" The little dog in the back of the barrel pig cart sat erect inside his fuzzy sock, staring directly at Mr. Friendle. Who did he think he was kidding, hiding inside that rust bucket suit of armour? Sir was about to become an inspector, there was no pussy footing around now!

Mr. Friendle felt ill. He thought back to earlier that afternoon when he had taken sweet Remoh home after her piano lessons and the miserable devious Horrible had come back into town, slithered his way into the music shop uninvited, and made it understood that if Mr. Friendle didn't follow through with their despicable plan to help destroy the young Gypsy girl's life, that Horrible would make bacon out of Hubert and Humphrey, demolish his prized metal piano and, lowest of all, would take his sweetheart Remoh and abandon her in the mountains.

It sickened Mr. Friendle to know that he was part of a dastardly plan to destroy this sweet Gypsy girl's life. But he couldn't stand to lose his cherished pigs, and heaven forbid anything happen to his one and only beautiful metal piano, so he carried on as though nothing was going to happen. As they got closer to the town, Friendle started to slow down his pigs. He knew Remoh was waiting at the ball for him and what would she think of him now? Sadly, everything else became more important than the sweet Gypsy girl's life. But he knew his freedom was at stake, unfortunately the desperate Mr. Friendle was a big part of a despicable plan.

Sir's eyeballs protruded from his head as he saw the town before him. They rode towards the entrance of the gigantic knight, where flames rose high from its huge metal mouth piece. From a large metal glove hung a red-hot ball of fire inside a flail. Pieces of hot ash fell upon the ground. The heat moved inside the metal knight's body, it glowed and crawled as though it had a life of its own. Mr. Friendle rode between the V-shape of the knight's large steel legs, where blazing fire burned high from its inseams.

Flames of green and purple roared high from the top of the knight's helmet. His huge metal chest glowed orange from the heat. Valena looked up. She could see sweat pouring from the Gatemaster's face as he stared down at them, then the big chains banged and scraped together and the heavy glowing chest of the giant knight opened for them to enter. As Mr. Friendle steered his two pigs through the entrance, Valena pulled her mask from her cloak sleeve and put it over her eyes.

The smell of smoke filled the damp night air as fires burned high into the night from the rooftops of the rusted metal homes. Valena gazed out of the small eye openings of her mask. The corsages that she had grown in her own garden were being worn by everyone. Brightly lit torches sat in large barrels of dirt and lined the main street. People came from all over the land to attend this great celebration. Valena saw so many beautiful costumes and charming hairstyles. As Mr. Friendle's pigs pulled his strange barrelled cart through the town, Sir's alert dog eyes were watching everything. Sitting under one of the food tables they passed by was the dirty little white cat Sir had been in pursuit of all day, she noticed him as well and deliberately darted across the street in front of them. Sir instantly jumped out of the carriage and the chase was on. In a split second the cat was up a tree; Sir ran in, jumped at the tree, and started barking like crazy at the antagonistic feline.

"Sir!" Valena cried loudly, then quickly covered her mouth remembering that she was not supposed to be there.

The cat comfortably settled herself about eight feet above the ground on a low branch, looking down smugly at Sir in his fuzzy grey sock, still barking foolishly.

"Oh! That silly dog always goes missing at the most inconvenient times," Valena complained.

Just then Mr. Friendle pulled his barrelled carriage over to the side of the street.

"I'll drop you off here, just follow the cobblestone path and you will get to a big stage where all the contestants are going to be waiting to take part in the Hair Ball," said Mr. Friendle nervously. "I'm going to find Remoh now. She will be wandering about trying to recognize my voice."

"Thank you for the ride," said Valena apprehensively. She got out of Mr. Friendle's carriage and started to head in toward the festivities.

Mr. Friendle, feeling ill at ease, carried on to tie his pigs to a nearby tree when he suddenly got a tremendous idea. He would hide his pigs in case things didn't go exactly as planned. Untying his precious pigs from their barrel, he led them across the cobblestone street and into the town's small cemetery. He knew that there were a few five-foot-deep pre-dug graves in the back of the property and his big pigs would be safe inside one, so he pushed Humphrey in first. The fat hairy pig landed with a thud and grunted. Next Mr. Friendle pushed Hubert, who was even fatter and uncooperative. He bounced against Humphrey and became wedged tightly between the earth and Humphrey's big belly. The two big hairy pigs looked up at Mr. Friendle like he was going to kill them. They balled like babies, tears streamed down to the ends of their big wrinkled snouts, their bellies pressed together like rising bread dough.

"Method of Love," Friendle repeated as he took off his rusted metal boot, filled it with dead leaves a few times and dumped them down onto the pigs backs to hide them. Quickly putting his boot back on, dear Mr.

Friendle's costume rattled while making his way back out of the graveyard. Heading towards the party to find Remoh, he was nervously looking around to make sure no one had been watching him when he banged his rusty suit of junk right into the gleaming suit of armour being worn by the wicked Horrible Horribin.

"In a hurry to go somewhere?" Horrible asked abruptly, brandishing his mean-looking sword.

Friendle cleared his throat and in a rather high voice that echoed from inside his rusty helmet, asked, "A real sword?"

"Yes, lovely and sharp, and made of steel," boasted Horrible, while pasting a sick smile to his face. He then took the point of his sword and leaned it on Mr. Friendle's rusted boot. It caused the rusted toe piece to crumble off with a crunch. Underneath Mr. Friendle's helmet was the face of a man that went ten shades of red.

"And where, may I ask, is the lovely Miss Valena on this special night?" demanded Horrible, tapping Mr. Friendle's rusted kneecap which broke off and fell to the ground.

Feeling embarrassed by this whole ordeal, Mr. Friendle reassured Horrible that everything was going to go as planned.

"Valena will be up on stage with the rest of the contestants, won't she, Friendle?" asked Horrible in a threatening tone.

Mr. Friendle shook his helmet in a yes motion, moving slightly away. Just then his rusty old sword's handle broke off and fell to the ground. He hung his head to see where it had landed when the mouth piece of his old corroded knight's helmet broke off on one side and hung swinging by the hinge. All he really cared about now was that his pigs were safe.

"Excellent," replied Horrible, hurrying to carry on with the rest of his evil plan.

Meanwhile, back in the little cemetery, Hubert and Humphrey were getting irritated from being wedged together in the tight space. They were snorting to beat the band when Humphrey's eyes suddenly bulged out of his head and, with a muffled sound, he passed gas. It stank. He enjoyed the reaction it got from Hubert, who was offended and started grunting loudly. He pushed himself up against Humphrey to warn him to mind his manners when out came another huge blast of gas. Hubert squealed, then Humphrey squealed, their eyes bulged wide as they pushed up against each other. Dirt fell from the walls of the earthy grave and the camouflage of leaves fell from their backs, exposing them to the full moonlight. Then they both became silent when they heard a scratching sound from up above the grave. Suddenly something white and fluffy jumped down onto Humphrey's back. He squealed as a set of sharp claws dug into him and a scary sound pierced both pig's big hairy ears.

"Meooooooow!" screeched the white hairy pouncing object. It frightened the pigs half to death. Then it jumped over onto Hubert's back and scratched him, its two big wild kaleidoscope eyes glowed from within the darkness of the grave. The white furry cat jumped out and took off, Hubert and Humphrey thought they'd been attacked by a ghost.

Now Shway had been wandering around, staring at all the costumes, and was half way to the judges table to do his job when he heard pigs squealing over in the graveyard.

He decided to go in and take a look around. He followed the sound, singing and skipping between the grave stones like the idiot that he was. Finally he looked down into one of the partially pre-dug graves and saw Mr. Friendle's pigs squished together with a look of terror upon their porky faces. He speculated that they had probably wandered onto the grounds and accidentally fallen into the grave because it was so dark. The pigs looked at each other then up at Shway, who was dressed as a princess. Neither of the pigs were amused but they pretended his costume was a little appealing and gave their best pig grins so Shway would want to save them. Sliding down inside the grave he slipped underneath them, getting pig droppings stuck to his costume, then, squeezing his tall limber body between them, he pushed Humphrey out first. Then he helped Hubert out. He finally crawled out himself, his costume was filthy dirty and smelled of pig droppings. The two big hairy pigs laughed at him.

"I know you're happy, you're welcome, now, shoo!" Shway yelled. He watched them waddle their rotund bodies through the grounds. They headed out towards the cobblestone way, towards some of the people who were enjoying the party. Humphrey headed straight for a food table and helped himself to some maple fudge that got stuck all over his snout, he slobbered on the ground. Hubert found a dripping spout on a keg of purpleberry tonic and licked it as much as he could, then let out a huge belch. Then they traded places, both becoming quite intoxicated, their stomachs bulging as they staggered about, finally sprawling under a tree where a random guest became scared by them and screamed in disgust, calling them slobbering pigs.

Meanwhile Shway had headed back towards the party with damp earth and stinky pig droppings stuck to his clothing. He walked proudly, feeling like a hero for saving the pigs. He took his place at the judges table just in time, for Horrible was walking angrily straight towards him, wondering where he'd been. Meanwhile, Mr. Friendle was also coming that way and was returning from hiding a special box of chocolates inside his piano to surprise his sweetheart, Remoh. He was sauntering around looking for her, feeling in a rather romantic mood, until he saw Horrible talking with one of the judges who was odd and looked different from the other women. She was wearing a long pink dress that was too small for her and was stained with brown spots, it had a crumpled dirty red bow tied high on the waist. On her large hands were short filthy lace gloves and sitting crookedly on top of her long blonde hair was a dainty, bent tiara. It wasn't until Mr. Friendle saw some hairy legs in a pair of boots underneath the table that he realized it was Shway.

Oh dear, thought Friendle to himself, looking as though he'd smelled a rotten egg.

"Shway, I see you found the costume I left for you," laughed Horrible. "It's filthy you IDIOT! Just…judge?"

"Do you like my corsage? Is my lipstick on straight?" Shway asked, imitating a woman's voice.

"I would concentrate on winning a real wig if I were you," Horrible said, insulting his accomplice. That wasn't very funny Shway thought to himself, twirling his long hair with the pointer finger of one dirty glove while primping at his bent tiara with the other one, to keep his wig in place.

As Valena walked through the party she noticed long wooden tables decorated with bouquets of lovely fresh flowers that she had grown in her garden. She felt honoured. The tables were decorated with fresh rose petals delicately scattered around trays of delicious food and desserts. In the middle of another table was a strange huge cake. The bottom was iced with dark grey icing that looked like a dress in the shape of a cone. On the top of it sat the head of a doll with long black hair that had been dusted with silver glitter, and beside it was a large sharp knife to cut the cake. There were some people standing in a small group drinking purpleberry punch, talking and laughing. Valena overheard one woman say that this year was more special than any of the others and hoped she would get to cut the cake.

Valena had never imagined such a party in her life. Trying to conceal her identity, she moved slowly through the crowd. She came upon a table with a sign that read: First Prize. On a stand sat a beautiful wig of real soft human hair. She touched it. It was the most beautiful hair she had ever felt. If only I had hair this lovely, she thought to herself. Everyone seemed to be having a great time. As Valena looked about she could see a most dazzling costume, the person in it was walking straight towards her. She felt nervous for she hadn't run into Horrible yet this evening and couldn't imagine what kind of a costume he would be wearing. Suddenly a knight in a golden suit stood beside her, the shine from the armour was blinding. The knight had a big gold sword. Engraved on the chest of the suit was a pear-sized lace heart. Valena didn't move. The person inside the gold armour opened the mouth piece and spoke to her.

"Hello," said Benjamin, his kind voice echoing from within the helmet.

"Hello, nice to meet you," answered Valena.

"You look beautiful in your feathered mask," he said.

"Thank you, and you look very…shiny, in your golden knight's armour," said Valena.

"Valena, it's me, Benjamin."

"Oh, I didn't recognize you."

"That's why we wear costumes," he replied.

"Oh, I don't have a costume," said Valena. "I only have a mask. Your mother asked if I was coming tonight!"

"She didn't mention that to me. She told me she didn't feel well and couldn't be here this time, but wished me a wonderful evening," said the prince.

"The queen is very kind, I hope she feels better soon," Valena said.

"Are you in the competition?" Benjamin asked.

"Ah...no, I mean I could be, well, yes," said Valena bravely.

"It sure is warm inside this shiny suit," said Benjamin.

"You look charming," Valena said, complementing him.

They heard a deep voice interrupt them from behind.

"You look charming," said Horrible, coming up to them and mocking his nephew.

"Thank you," replied Benjamin sarcastically.

"You have such a wit about you, my nephew," Horrible sneered. "Miss Valena, are you ready to join the other contestants?" Horrible invited her politely.

"Yes, I'm ready," Valena answered, looking about nervously.

"No! Your hair is already beautiful. Give the other girls a chance to win," Benjamin urged.

"Why, Benjamin, I'm shocked. Of all the people to take away a beautiful young girl's dream, the chance to win first prize and have fun," Horrible challenged in a cunning voice.

Benjamin slid his hand onto his golden sword handle. It hung majestically from his chained belt.

"Run along, Valena, and get up on stage with all the other contestants," Horrible encouraged her. Valena left their company and headed towards the pathway that led her to the big stage where there was a long line of contestants waiting. She felt queasy and nervous and didn't know how the hairdressers would ever get her strange hair cut off.

Meanwhile Remoh had found her seat on the right hand side of the stage where she knew Mr. Friendle's piano was situated. She sat there every year so she could hear the man who had inspired her to play the piano. She waited patiently, any time now the contest was going to begin, and Mr. Friendle would play the opening piece on his famous metal piano. This beautiful sound hugged Remoh's heart, there was nothing in the world like Oscar Friendle's fingers playing upon his metal grand piano. Remoh tucked in the sides of her lovely dress as she sat upon the wooden bench. She reached to her hair to make sure her lovely royal red orchid was in just the right place, in case Mr. Friendle was to notice how she was dressed. Her orchid was missing, it had fallen off somewhere she thought to herself. She felt her lap, then leaned over and felt around the ground by her feet. Suddenly her delicate hands felt a pair of cold metal boots, she worked her hands upward upon the metal structure until she was sitting up straight again.

"Lose something?" Horrible said.

"Erick! Is that you?" Remoh asked,

"You have a wonderful ear!" Horrible remarked.

Remoh became silent, she knew her brother was always up to no good. So she tried to make the conversation short.

"I've lost my red orchid, that Valena gave me."

"Oh dear, I spotted it by the stage earlier. I knew it was yours, I saw you wearing it when you came in. I'll take you to it, I'm positive it's yours," Horrible said, his mind churning.

Maybe Erick had changed and he was trying to be helpful, Remoh thought to herself, and so she got up and went with him to find her pretty orchid. Horrible took his sister gently by the arm and guided her to the side of the stage and made light conversation.

"Nice night," Horrible said.

"Yes, I'm anxious to hear Mr. Friendle play his beautiful piano," Remoh said.

"I'm willing to make sure you hear him much better than the rest of the crowd." Then, once they had gone around the side of the stage where no one could see them, horrid Horrible grabbled his sister's arm and tossed her walking stick away, then shoved her sideways right underneath the stage.

"Here's your seat! Right here! Below your sweetheart," Horrible proclaimed, clutching her arm and pulling her to the exact spot below where Mr. Friendle's piano was sitting above her on the stage.

"If this plan fails, you die!" Horrible told her, roughly untying the pretty bow on the back of her dress. He took the long untied strands and tightly tied them around a long horizontal wooden board which was part of the stage frame so Remoh could hardly breathe, then he yanked the pretty scarf from the top of her damsel cone hat and tied it around her mouth so she couldn't scream.

"I'm going to become THE KING tonight little sister," he proclaimed. "Enjoy the party!" He poked the end of Remoh's nose with his cold bony pointer finger.

"The Gypsy girl's head will be my trophy tonight!" Horrible boasted, then he left her there alone in the cold dampness under the stage and went back to his event.

Remoh shook in fear, her eyes bulged from their sockets. She screamed but the noise from the large crowd muffled any sound she was making. She could hear the contestants walking around on the stage above her, then, as the great Oscar Friendle began to play his most famous piece of music, Remoh cried.

It was Valena's turn. She stepped out of the contestants lineup, she was afraid to go on stage. She adjusted her mask then remembered what the Quimmies had told her—the mask would give her strength—so she lined up again and slowly went up the stairs. When she had reached the top she walked across the floor of the stage nervously. She saw a tall man pull out a chair and motion for her to sit down. When all the contestants were seated the competition was well in session. Each contestant had their own hairdresser, some better than others. Valena could see the crowd watching them with anticipation. From where she sat she could see Rosey and Posey standing not far from a tree where Kermack was tied. Thank goodness they weren't paying attention. They were talking to a large white cat. Yikes, thought Valena, they know Zeezee too? I hope she doesn't tell them she's met me.

Zeezee turned her head from Rosey and Posey and gave Valena a wink of her kaleidoscope eye. She was doing well by keeping the two women busy so they wouldn't notice Valena up on the stage.

"Your costume is extremely authentic," Rosey complimented Zeezee.

"Yes," added Posey sweetly.

"I find both of yours very unexplainable," the cat said in a superior manner, "yet mine is rather purr-fect."

"Who invited the cat!" snapped Rosey, giving Zeezee a dirty look, then pulling her sister by the arm and waltzing away in a huff. Zeezee sauntered off through the crowd, passing right through them in a ghost-like state. Valena saw this from up on the stage and was shocked, she was worried about Sir and wondered where he was. Then she noticed that Remoh was gone from her seat and Horrible had taken her place. Valena began to feel frightened, her hair began to get warm.

Prince Benjamin had wandered through the crowd and stood way back beneath a large oak tree. A cool wind blew gently, it was a beautiful autumn evening. He removed his heavy knight's helmet to get a better look at lovely Valena on the stage. His pupils grew large as he gazed at her, he became mesmerized, spellbound, and began to fantasize. He imagined holding her tenderly in his strong arms, her long beautiful silver and black shiny hair falling out from her hooded cloak and laying upon the shoulder of his gold suit of armour, her cape flowing gracefully as they slowly waltzed together amongst the shadows of the trees in the moonlit forest. He moved his head towards hers and became lost in a sweet innocent wonderland of love, his imagination filled his mind with a stream of romantic thoughts.

Light the secret candle, the one in my heart,
'twas true love from the very start.
Her hair of silver, eyes of desire,
mesmerized my soul and set it on fire.
Her mystical grace, her white wild honey face,
will take us to a magical place.
Where dragons graze and knights are bold,
and stories of romance remain untold.
Upon this moonlit night I see,
a beautiful Gypsy girl for me.
A distant rain storm, a luminous rainbow from
the sun,
this heart of mine she has surely won.
A magical spell, a dance in time,
with each beat of my heart I will make her
mine.

With a loud thud the prince's heavy gold helmet hit the ground, frightening him back into reality. His body was hot, his head had broken into a sweat, he had never felt like this before. Greatly embarrassed he bent down and picked up his helmet, then looked around to see if anyone had noticed. With a puzzled look upon his face he looked up at the moon, he had never seen it like this before, it was an eerie sight—a full moon with the form of a sleeping Gypsy queen upon it. He recalled Remoh telling him stories when he was a young boy, about how if one saw a sleeping Gypsy queen upon the moon, the dead Gypsy king's ghost was coming back and would haunt the land, longing for his Gypsy queen who had died a gruesome death hundreds of years ago. Benjamin shivered and patted the handle of his sword then remembered this was only one of Remoh's many silly ghost stories. Then he put his helmet on and walked back into the crowd to watch the competition. On his way he noticed Mr. Friendle had left the stage and joined some of the men over at the strongest knight competition, throwing big rocks into a barrel of water that was many yards away from them. They all were trying to win big prizes. He thought it was strange that Remoh was not anywhere around so he walked closer to the stage, but still he couldn't see her. Then he saw Horrible sitting in her place, watching Valena.

Valena's hairdresser had slid her cloak hood from her head. He'd been cutting her hair for quite some time now with no luck, and was even pulling at it to get it to come off. All the jostling about caused the crystal ball to accidentally fall out of Valena's cloak pocket, the eerie Gypsy moon activated the titanium flower inside of it and it glowed brightly as it rolled across the stage floor. Everyone saw this. Valena ran to pick it up and put it back in her pocket. Horrible had seen this and it solidified the fact that she was the Gypsy princess. He got up from where he was sitting and walked over to the judges table and handed Shway a secret note to give to Valena's hairdresser. It read, CUT OFF HER HEAD. Shway left the judges table to deliver the message but a human-sized white scruffy cat bumped his arm and he dropped the note on the ground, amongst the crowd of people. He panicked and ran away like a little child, hiding underneath the back of the stage in fear. He looked out toward the back field and could see his tubby new red cob horse, who he had named Lucky, helping herself to some apples that were floating in a barrel of water. While Shway sat underneath the stage he looked around and saw something white and orange. He thought it was a ghost. His eyes widened as he adjusted them to the darkness and he saw it was someone tied to the wooden structure, and they were gagged. Shway bent at the waist, ducked his head, and walked slowly on the mucky ground. He slipped, then got up and, with his long gangly legs, he climbed over the boarded structure that held the stage up. Finally he reached the person that had looked like a ghost. He looked closely at her, she struggled as he removed her pretty mask.

"Renew! Re...gew!" he said, snapping his fingers in front of his face. "Wait, I...I know, Re...Re...MOH!" Shway squawked, then quickly covered his mouth with his big hand. He remembered her from years before when he was a young man and lived in the castle, and he knew she was partially blind. Remoh looked terrified and was tossing her head around like a wild horse, trying to get the scarf off of her mouth. Shway looked at her frightened face and gently removed the scarf. Remoh let out a scream, so he covered her mouth back up again.

"No, no, no, don't scream," said Shway, shaking his long wig of princess hair.

"It's Shway, remember me?" he said, removing his wig. Then, like the dunce that he was, he curtsied and bowed as though Remoh could see him.

"I remember. You're Horrible's sister, the princess that can't see!" Shway whispered. "I can't help you. Shh…" he continued, "your brother might hear us. He's out there sitting centre stage, I heard him yelling something!"

Remoh nodded her head up and down indicating, yes, you can help me. Tears rolled from the corners of her squinting eyes. Shway decided to remove the scarf from her cold clammy mouth.

"Horrible gave your father his vest and lied to the king, who unknowingly sentenced an innocent man. Now Horrible is going to kill an innocent girl!" cried Remoh.

"The Gatemaster is innocent too!" Shway told Remoh.

"He is?" asked Remoh. Shway had spotted Remoh's walking stick, he went over and picked it up off the mucky ground then gently put it in her hand.

"Yes, Horrible and I burned the Gypsy village down and smashed the walls too!" Shway said, crossing his arms on his chest and nodding his head in a 'yes, we did!' motion. "And we kidnapped the Gatemaster. He's not really bad, he's just a Gypsy that can't talk so he could never tell anyone what we had done, and that we were looking to steal the Gypsy queen's heirloom locket necklace. But she hid it real good, and we still can't find it," Shway told her in his dunce-like manner.

"Oh my. Oh, we have to help Valena," said Remoh.

Shway thought for a moment then a light bulb went off in his slow-witted brain. He decided his friendship with Horrible was over and he untied Remoh.

"You get behind me under my dress and

hang on to my undershorts," Shway told her. Remoh blushed. The idea of his undershorts embarrassed her, but she composed herself and under she went. Being petite she fit perfectly. Funny enough, it smelled like pig droppings under there so Remoh tried not to breath in too deeply and thought to herself, royalty or not, this was an emergency. Then they snuck out from under the stage and, wobbling together, they tried to hide while mingling amongst the crowd as they headed toward the tower of the big knight, where Garth was. Shway had his own simple plan in place.

Now, all seven of the hair dressers were cutting as fast as they could. Benjamin watched intensely and noticed that Valena's hairdresser had broken all his scissors. Silver strands of her hair began to glimmer in the full moonlight. The threads of hair on her mask began to glow as well. Horrible glared at her with vengeance in his eyes. The hairdresser was angry and couldn't cut off even one piece of Valena's strong hair. Horrible was getting really antsy and wondered what had happened to his note—why was it taking so long for the message to get to the hairdresser?

"Her hair is dirty, it won't cut," the hairdresser hissed at Horrible, holding a razor above her head.

Horrible realized then that the hairdresser had not received his note. He screamed at the hairdresser in so much panic and desperation, the man dropped his razor.

"Cut. Off. Her. Head!"

"My head!" Valena yelled, as she stood up quickly and pulled her mask down to her neck so she could see better. Zeezee was right, she thought, the bad man wants my head. Valena was frightened, her hair and eyelashes glowed brightly. As her eyes transformed into purple kaleidoscopes, they cast purple laser beams as she glared down upon the crowd. Finding Horrible Horribin, she fixated on him then pointed him out.

"That man!" she screamed as loud as she could. "He's a bad horrible man."

The crowd gasped in fear, Benjamin was jolted out of his blissful reverie, and Rosey and Posey stood in shock. The crowd began to grumble loudly, Horrible pushed through them towards the stage. Benjamin went into a state of alert and grabbed his gold sword.

"Get her!" Horrible yelled loudly, reaching for his heavy sword.

Valena bolted across the stage, tripping over the other contestants, and jumped off the edge of it, landing right on Rosey and Posey's cart. She ripped the reins from the tree and yelled at old Kermack, "LETS GO." Suddenly the dirty little white cat with glowing whiskers fell from a tree into the back of the cart, her kaleidoscope eyes burned at the sight of Horrible Horribin racing for his horse.

"Go, Kermack, go!" yelled Valena over the noise in the crowd.

Benjamin ran as fast as he could through the crowd to get to his horse.

As Kermack ran recklessly, his heavy body knocked over the first prize table and a wig landed right on top of his head. He shook it off then rammed into the food tables, food flew through the air and landed all over the people and onto the ground. Kermack also wiped out the big strange looking cake, sending it sailing high into the air, splattering all over Rosey and Posey's weird costumes. Kermack caused a disastrous mess.

He couldn't remember the last time he had moved that fast.

Kermack and Valena were heading towards the raging inferno of the giant knight.

Horrible lifted up his chin piece.

"Close the gate!" he demanded loudly, as he mounted his huge black stallion. "Shway! Where is that idiot?" He turned his horse toward the tower. "Close the knight, you crazy fool!" he shouted to the Gatemaster, then spurred his horse hard in the girth in hot pursuit of the fleeing Valena.

Garth looked down from his position in the tower, his hard work had paid off. Years of tension on one specific link in the chain had caused it to break so now the huge chain would not close the big heavy door, it just fell and twisted rapidly, falling downward like a metal rattlesnake. The joining chains that bound Garth came off, the cuff bands remained but he was a free man. Looking down he saw some woman in a princess dress motioning him to come down.

He quickly climbed down the side of the tower. For some reason he saw a six-foot-long ghost-like chain attached to his right ankle cuff. The ancient Gypsy ghost curse had gotten worse! I'm wearing the Gypsy king's ghost chain! But why? Garth thought to himself. He couldn't feel the weight of it, but as he walked it dragged behind him, making a loud sound on the ground. Strange, he thought.

Garth walked over to where Shway was standing, slightly bent at the waist.

"Horrible is gonna kill Valena. He's gonna kill her," Shway repeated himself nervously. Remoh appeared, timidly, from underneath the back of his dress.

Garth recognized them even in costume and acknowledge the information.

"Valena…what a pretty name?" Garth thought to himself, in a daze.

"You can have my horse, she's really fast," boasted Shway.

As Shway led the way, Garth took Remoh's hand and they all went through the crowd on the side of the streets. It took them a while to get to Shway's fat cob horse, and also a while to get it moving as it was still eating apples. Garth helped Remoh up onto the big animal, then he got on the horse and they took off fast after everyone. He was determined to save his daughter's life. Shway stayed back in the town.

Hearing the confusion, Sir, who was situated high up in the tower of the giant knight, had been spying on the Gatemaster and getting a good view of the celebration. He was startled to see Valena in the flower cart, racing Kermack straight for the open gate of the giant knight as fast as she could, followed by Horrible Horribin rapidly galloping after her on his horse and, immediately after that, Benjamin racing on his horse in pursuit of Horrible. Then the townspeople, with lit torches, came racing through on their horses after him. Sir gulped. There was no time to think. He jumped. Sir came gliding down through the scorching heat, like a leaf on a hot wind, and landed with a loud thump onto the seat beside Valena.

"Sir, where have you been?" she cried.

"It's getting hotter and hotter in this ridiculous costume, this wool sock you put me in," he complained, doing a tuck and roll for safety reasons, then catching his balance and wiping the sweat from his brow. He looked back. Horrible Horribin was catching up to them.

"I think it would be a good idea if you put on a little speed," Sir advised Valena. "If you know what I mean."

"Go, Kermack! Go faster!" she yelled.

Kermack ran like he never ran before and they headed towards the forest.

Horrible was catching up to her and Benjamin's horse was close behind him. Poor Mr. Friendle, who had earlier failed to find his sweetheart Remoh, had gone with Rosey and Posey. His pigs were staggering to keep up with the crowd. The whole town was racing

towards the forest after Valena and Horrible Horribin.

"We have to hide in the forest," said Valena.

"We? Really? Are you sure?" said Sir.

Luckily he hadn't noticed the cat riding down low in back of the cart.

Valena rode Kermack hard, he ran like a race horse, his mane glowed in the moonlight and his head was held high.

"I didn't think the old boy had it in him, he looks rather heroic tonight," Sir said in a complimentary fashion, wondering what was going on.

"Now, look what trouble you've gotten us into, Sir," Valena said.

"It's your hair they want, not mine," he said, glad to be balding.

The sleeping Gypsy moon shone brightly down upon them and shadows raced along the ground. Off in the distance the mighty castle of Zymurgy was darkened. Fog floated about the tombstones up in the old graveyard. At last Valena could see the forest up ahead. Kermack took Valena off the road, charging through the darkness of the huge trees like a bolt of lightning. Valena couldn't see anything but Kermack steered the cart up a path that took them straight into the big ancient uprooted tree stump, and crashed. Valena flew from the top of the cart and hit her head on a large hardened exposed root, knocking her unconscious. The dirty little white cat sprang off the cart and ran down by a pond, disappearing into the woods. Sir hung on for dear life but was thrown to the ground. He quickly got up, with a big lump on his head, and ran over to where Valena lay. She didn't move. Sir couldn't bear it as she lay on the ground motionless. He barked at her and licked her face, trying to bring her to consciousness, but nothing worked. The button from her hooded cloak had been ripped off and the cape lay loosely around her neck. The glow from the silver strands of her mask faded as it lay crookedly on her neck. Sir could hear the thundering sounds of horses racing into the forest and people yelling, their torches scorched the trees. Up inside the roots of the hollow tree stump floated an eerie grey mist, which cast a muted light down upon them.

Horrible's huge horse was the first to enter the hollow tree where Valena's body lay. Steam rose from his big black stallion. Benjamin arrived next, his handsome black and white cob horse bolted in and halted a few feet from his uncle's. Mr. Friendle and his hairy pigs rode in with Rosey and Posey, they all jumped out of the barrel quickly and went into the big tree stump. Then the people of the town rode in, got down off their horses, and gathered just at the entrance of the ancient hollow tree, struggling to see this strange young girl who lay on the cold ground.

Horrible rode up beside Valena's still body, got down from his horse and removed his heavy knight's helmet, placing it on the ground beside him, then drew his sword as he slowly came back up. He slid the point of it under one of Valena's limp wrists and lifted it up off the ground, letting it fall back to the damp earth. He didn't know whether she was dead or alive.

"My, my, what do we have here? Tisk, tisk, what a shame, what a waste," he sneered, as spit was forced through his dirty rotten teeth.

He knelt down and carefully pulled apart the collar of her dress. Horrible studied her, she was beautiful. There, around her thin pale neck, was what Horrible had been looking for all these years—the beautiful Gypsy heirloom Knight of Wishhearts locket and titanium chain. He gently lifted her head enough to slip it off. Then he got to his feet, turned, and glared at Benjamin.

"Benjamin, my dear nephew, is it not true that if you possess the beautiful locket necklace and behead a Ecae Gypsy princess on the night of her sixteenth birthday, you will become the most powerful knight in all the land?"

Benjamin got down from his horse, keeping his eyes fixed upon his uncle. He wanted to pull his sword but he controlled himself as a master knight had taught him.

"But, you have the locket necklace, what more could you want?"

"Riches, strength, wisdom, and most of all—power! I'm going to have it all!" Horrible proclaimed with a dastardly laugh.

Then he gazed with admiration at the beautiful Gypsy locket necklace in his hand.

"I will have you know," Sir spoke out

loudly as he backed away from the tyrant, his legs trembling, "that...that's not yours!"

"Silence! It's all mine, mine, mine!" Horrible said greedily, putting the necklace around his neck. Then he lifted his sword with a flourish.

"I am the king of this village now, and I command the great Gypsy powers to give me all the titanium that this land has to offer." Sliding his sword back into its sheath, Horrible waited for his command to be fulfilled. Nothing happened. He was breathing heavily from his dark anger. He slipped the Gypsy heirloom from his neck and with his left clenched fist held it high above his head, shaking it desperately.

"Give me my titanium that I have waited for all these years!" he roared.

In the distance came the sound of rapid horse hooves approaching and the dragging of a heavy pounding chain. No one moved, everyone stood afraid.

"It's the ghost of the Gypsy king finally coming for his dead Gypsy queen!" Posey cried out.

The people of the town were terrified.

Even Horrible froze in dreadful anticipation. Then bolting into the big hollow tree stump, a big red cob horse headed straight for Horrible, who turned in terror. It was Garth, astride Shway's horse, with Remoh hanging on behind him for dear life. With his right hand Horrible grabbed for his sword, but just as he did, Garth grabbed Remoh's walking stick and swung it towards Horrible, it hooked the locket necklace out of his left hand and flung it up into the air to fall deep into the dark cold water of the nearby pond. Horrible grabbed his helmet, put it on and exploded into a fit of rage, lifting his sword with both hands and, with all his might, plunged it down to cut off Valena's head. But the titanium hair mask that lay across her neck was harder and stronger than his sword, which bounced off with a loud sharp ring. With the anger of a giant breathing with the heavy rattling of defeat, Horrible turned to Benjamin with murderous intent blazing in his eyes, then, lifting his sword, Horrible lunged toward him. Benjamin stepped back quickly, Horrible lunged again. Benjamin stepped back even more, luring his uncle to the edge of the giant tree, where the pond lay just ten feet below. With a hot battle cry Horrible sliced his sword across Benjamin's forearm, but in the heavy swinging motion he stumbled. In a flash Benjamin struck his uncle's sword, sending it flying up into the tree roots. The Quimmies grabbed it. Now the Tainted Knight backed away, cautiously, in terrible fear, his gleaming eyes watched Benjamin come towards him. Horrible retreated another step backward and stumbled again. Benjamin came up close to him, put the flat of his sword against his uncle's chest and pushed. Horrible fell backwards, down into the deep pond. He screamed for help for he couldn't swim and his heavy knight's armour quickly sank him, bubbling down into the dark cold murky water until he disappeared.

Benjamin turned and walked away from the ugly sight. However, unbeknownst to anyone, Horrible—that evil Tainted Knight—got lucky and caught the toe of his boot on a piece of the Gypsy wall that had fallen down into the pond many years ago. The flat of his foot stood exactly where the heirloom locket's chain had hung itself earlier, and where the locket now dangled in the murky water. Unaware of this, the Tainted Knight clung to the wall and, kicking his feet to get out of the water, saved himself from drowning. In so doing he knocked the heirloom locket and chain right off the ledge, sending it deeper into the pond. He soon climbed out after shedding his heavy metal suit which, like a tortuous shell, sank deep into the murky pond water. Horrible scrambled out in his dripping undergarments and climbed a high tree to hide above the pond area, soaking wet. He covered himself with some tree branches that still had a few leaves left on them, his eyesight was blurred from the slimy pond water and he couldn't see much of anything.

There at the bottom of the pond lay the beautiful locket and chain. It had settled at once onto another piece of the wall, a special piece that lay at the bottom of the pond. It was upon this small ledge that, many long years ago when the first Gypsy queen was a newborn, imprints of the right and left palms of her hands were made—as was the custom—onto a secretly formulated titanium mortar that had been inlaid onto the ledge. Now, deep in the dark water of the pond, the Gypsy heirloom locket lay gently cupped in these imprints. It was believed among the Gypsies that these imprints had a mystical and magical property, and that a day of reformation would come to bring back the celebration of Ecae day and a new Gypsy princess to reign and one day become the queen.

The townspeople were quiet as they watched Prince Benjamin bow his head in sadness. Then a mournful moaning sound echoed from up inside Silver Mountain where the Mipsie ghost's cocoons were stirring. They all stood, afraid. Suddenly an eerie dark purple steam rose from the cold ground beneath where the village once stood. The earth became warm and started to shift upward with thunderous sounds from under the earth, up rose the Gypsy village of Ecae. One by one each caravan appeared until the whole village came back, just as it was before the big fire had destroyed it. The wall with the children's palm imprints erupted from the ground and magically reconstructed itself once more around the village.

Lighting up the roots of the ancient tree

stump were the Quimmy Boinks. They hollered with joy as they were transformed back into the people who had lived in the village many years before. The magical spell slowly started to wear off.

Ecae day was about to begin.

The last caravan—the grandest of all with its soft pearl grey shine—began to rise up from beneath the warm ground. The magical home of Madam Teaspill now appeared where it had stood for many years before the fire. Kermack trotted over and stood in front of it, stoically, his coat gleamed of grey titanium metal and his mane dazzled with grey titanium sparkles. Everything came back, it was wonderful! What a great celebration it was going to be!

But, Valena, she still lay on the ground motionless.

"She's dead," said one little Gypsy girl, wiping her eyes on the cuff of her sleeve.

Inside that big old ancient tree stump everyone began to crowd in to take a closer look at Valena's lifeless body. Rosey and Posey were sobbing and in shock from what had happened. Everyone began to cry.

Everything had returned to the village, except Valena. Garth looked around for Isa, she hadn't come back either, then he looked around at the people—their faces were sad and their hearts broken. The last Gypsy princess was gone forever and now all that was left was an ordinary village, with people to fend for themselves. The magic of the village was lost, never to return again. Garth looked down at his beautiful daughter, her skin was starting to turn dull grey. In sadness he looked out beyond the big hollow tree towards his village, his mind raced, his heart beat hard. What keeps the Gypsy queen alive, what makes them see into the future, he wondered. Yes, their magic comes from their heirloom. Garth raised his head. The wooden heart, the metal frame—this thought flew like magic into his mind, he could hear the rushing of a waterfall in his head, something great was about to happen. Then he reached into his pocket and took out the metal frame with the intention of putting it back.

Just then Remoh got herself down from Shway's big cob horse, she put out her walking stick and found her way, the crowd parted and made a path for her to get through. Remoh called out for Benjamin who was kneeling by Valena's body while Sir lay by her head, for he loved her so. Big tears fell from Sir's sad round eyes.

Benjamin stood up slowly and walked straight to Remoh, as they met, she reached up and felt for the chain on his neck.

"The key!" exclaimed Benjamin.

Garth had stepped forward to join the prince and they ran fast back towards the centre of the village to Teaspill's caravan. Reaching the eerie pearl grey structure, Garth indicated to Benjamin with his hands that he had to climb up onto the top step of the caravan and put the metal frame back around the wooden heart-shaped compartment where it belonged. Benjamin then took the key from his neck and put it into the key-hole in the wooden heart. It magically turned and opened. Benjamin saw the titanium lace heart inside. It began to glow. He gently removed it and carried it carefully. Garth and Benjamin returned to Valena and the prince knelt down by her side, putting the beautiful glowing heart into her lifeless hand, which he kissed gently. Valena slowly opened her soft grey eyes and saw Prince Benjamin—the spell had been broken. As he knelt before her a beautiful shimmering patch of sweet peas appeared underneath her body then slowly moved up the side of the tree stump, forming itself into the shape of a lady waiting for someone. Valena began to stand up, then Isa's soft voice came mystically from the sweet peas, "Welcome home my little princess." Valena began transforming into a beautiful princess and her mask began to glow again, she put it over her eyes. Her hair became a veil of glowing titanium sweet peas. More glowing titanium sweet peas formed on her body in the shape of an elegant flowered dress, her flower-cuffed boots and gloves of titanium protected her delicate hands and feet.

Then, magically appearing into her right hand, was a heavy titanium sword, the handle of sweet peas in the shape of a 'V'. As she stood within the big tree stump Valena started to speak, and everyone watched her in admiration, for she was their Princess of Peace.

"This is the final sword, the last weapon that will ever exist throughout the land. We shall call it the Titanium Sword of Peace." Then, with a mighty force, Valena raised her sword high in the air and with both hands she drove it down deep into the ground, in the roots of the ancient tree stump.

"I am the Titanium Princess of Peace, the ruler of Ecaep," she proclaimed. "Be not afraid, I am here to show you how to change your world and give you hope so that all of you will share love and peace with one another wherever you go. You are free now."

"Hurray!" All the people of the village and of the town cheered and hugged one another.

In return for Garth's good deed the ancient Gypsy curse that had possessed him had been broken and, Garth realized, the rattling of the ghost chain was also gone, so with a puff of air he screamed along with all the others. His voice was weak but it had returned— after sixteen long years.

"Hurray! Hurray," he cried.

Then, a beautiful silence fell upon them and the weaponless Valena held her arms up over her head, crossing them with her palms out towards the people of her village as a sign of peace.

It was at that moment that the most miraculous thing happened to her for, on this special night of her sixteenth birthday, the new princess received a wonderful gift—the most important gift of all, one that no man could actually see—the transformation of her heart. For on that day Valena's transparent heart became filled with many beautiful colours. Soft yellow embraced a glowing red and the shimmer of black gleamed through bright pieces of white. She could feel a peacefulness inside herself and wanted to share it with everyone.

Benjamin stood beside his peaceful princess then lifted her hand to his lips and kissed it. Everyone in the village cheered. Sir ran circles around their feet then jumped right into Valena's arms and licked her nose.

"Hurray! Peace, peace!" they all shouted. "The Tainted Knight is gone FOREVER!"

Then Valena saw the dirty little white cat who dropped down from a huge tree. Valena smiled, then reached into her pocket and pulled out her crystal ball, the titanium sweet pea glowed brightly. She rolled the ball towards the cat who batted it about playfully until sparks magically flew from it, sending the crystal ball high up into the old worn out village sign which now read, ECAEP. The cat mystically disappeared into the night and as she did, a huge bonfire was lit in the centre of the village. Kermack, also a hero, wore his Gypsy medallion of honour proudly and it beamed radiant colourful rays of light that shot up into the dark night like a supernova. Excitedly, the families of the village gathered as one with the people of the town around the huge warm bonfire to celebrate Ecaep.

Valena and Benjamin walked over to the edge of the pond and removed the family heirloom—the Knight of Wishhearts locket—from the magical hand imprints in the wall. They placed the key and the titanium lace heart back inside the locket then Benjamin put the locket necklace around Valena's neck.

A flash of silver and purple light suddenly came from the top of Silver Mountain and the beautiful shimmering titanium waterfall began flowing once again. Prince Benjamin held Valena in his arms and kissed her on the lips as tiny specs of titanium sparkled around them in the moonlight.

Strangely, small rings formed in the pond water—droplets of water dripped from somewhere in the treetops. Valena put her hand out.

"Rain?" she questioned.

"It's just from the waterfall," Benjamin said, holding her close.

"Stupid Gypsies. I'll be back for MY titanium!" Horrible growled with a nasty scowl on his face, sitting unnoticed in the tree with his teeth chattering and his face getting paler and paler.

Benjamin and Valena were excited and soon returned to the celebration. There they were joined at the wrists with a big purple satin bow. They leaped over the bright white marriage flames of the Gypsy fire in their village tradition and lived peacefully ever after.

Oh, and the only one that wasn't there was Shway. He was still back in Metalville, which had turned into Petalville once again. He was trying desperately to win the Best Knight contest and get himself a brand new teddy bear.

ELEVEN

Gypsy

And so, Grandfather's story had finally come to an end. The tower room was now cold. He noticed that winter was upon them. He could see tiny snowflakes starting to fall outside the large stained glass window of the tower. His attention was brought towards a heavy wooden door that quietly crept open. A beautiful elderly woman entered the room. She carried a lit stained glass lantern and her small slippers patted the cool cobblestone floor as she quietly walked over to Grandfather's big old storytelling throne. She bent down, gently picked up her grandson, and kissed him on the forehead. He had been sprawled over his grandfather's lap and was fast asleep. Grandfather smiled at her lovingly. He whispered to her as she left the darkened room.

"Goodnight, Valena."

"Goodnight, Sire," said Valena, with a gentle grin. She then held her little grandson close to her heart and walked towards the door and went out.

King Benjamin sat for a minute more. His old cat Gypsy scurried out from under his chair and disappeared out the tower room doorway into the darkness. Strange old cat, he thought, you never know where she'll turn up next.

THE END

ABOUT THE AUTHOR

Norah McMenamon is a fantasy and fairy tale author whose passion is to entice the minds and hearts of the reader.

Norah can be found at any time surrounded by piles of paper, laughing or wiping her tears while she creates her stories with love. She lives in Pitt Meadows, British Columbia, Canada with her husband and three children. Norah has appeared on the American television series *Smallville*, and on the *Super Dave Osborne* show. Norah holds her certificates as a distinctive creative writer close to her heart, and has a diploma for film and television acting from a performing arts college in Vancouver, British Columbia.

CPSIA information can be obtained at www.ICGtesting.com
Printed in the USA
LVOW11*2033021115

460781LV00009B/20/P